FALLOUT

An Austin Cole Novel

BILL F. SELVIDGE

outskirtspress

DENVER, COLORADO

Fallout
An Austin Cole Novel
All Rights Reserved.
Copyright © 2014 Bill F. Selvidge
v2.0

Outskirts Press, Inc.
http://www.outskirtspress.com

ISBN: 978-1-4787-3810-7

Outskirts Press and the "OP" logo are trademarks belonging to Outskirts Press, Inc.

PRINTED IN THE UNITED STATES OF AMERICA

Dedications

To my wonderful wife who I know I don't deserve and without whom my life would be so empty, my soul and spirit would be unable to smile and surely my feet could not dance.

To my family, for their continuous support and encouragement. I can't thank you or love you enough. I am so blessed that my life shares part of yours.

To my friends for their energy, enthusiasm, amazing character and loyalty and in some cases over-the-top personality that have inspired me in ways I'm ill-equipped to describe.

To Sharon Coffman without whose creativity, effort and advice helped me pen what would have otherwise been a bumbling, inarticulate, inappropriately punctuated manuscript of which I'm sure I would have been profoundly embarrassed.

To all the men and women, either directly or indirectly associated with the Shuttle Columbia tragedy. I'm not capable of putting into words my admiration and appreciation for all you do and the grace with which you do it.

PROLOGUE

Saturday, February 1, 2003: 8:50 a.m.
Brookeland, Texas

Considering that it was only the first day of February it was beginning to look more like an early April morning than a winter's day with six more weeks to go until spring. The sun was shining brightly as though proudly taking credit for the cloudless, soft, blue sky. The wind was light and the temperature was only 47° as kids from the Brookeland Boy Scouts Troop 4 were eating breakfast made over the open fire. The anticipation of the temperature reaching 68° later that afternoon sparked a new optimism and sense of excitement for just about everyone as it promised to be a perfect day for hiking and sight-seeing. Spring fever was in the air and it threatened to develop into a full-blown epidemic.

By 7:30 a.m. each of the young men had packed up their gear and had already hiked about one half mile up the trail to the old Booker's Lookout, a popular spot with a great view and what was to be the end of their overnight camp out. They still had about 5 hours of hiking, climbing, wading, and skidding before they were expected to meet their parents at the lodge at the top, but each child was looking forward to the trip. After about an hour of hiking behind them the Scout leaders decided it was time for a 10 minute break, if not for the kids then at least for themselves. Several of the young men found larger rocks to sit on and lift their feet for a while. Others went down to the gently flowing mountain stream to wet a towel and wipe the sweat off their necks and forehead. The fact that the water was so cool was just an added bonus as the hike was making them work up a good sweat. Some of the kids merely lay back and basked in the sun, looking at the few clouds in an otherwise empty blue sky.

Danny Clark was lying on the ground with a small twig in his right hand pointing skyward and tracing little shapes against the backdrop of blue. Then, as his hands slowly floated to the ground, he sat upright and a look of bewilderment fell across his face. Sitting on the apex of a large bolder, Troop Leader Chad Owen kept a watchful eye on each of the kids as they found their respective areas to rest. As he surveyed the children he noticed Danny staring stoically into the blue.

Just as he was about to get up to go see what was wrong, Connor Brooks climbed up onto the stone beside him. Pointing upward he simply asked, "What's that?"

As Mr. Owen's gaze turned skyward he saw streaks of bright red and orange with grayish-white tails at the back end trailing across the blue sky. His words came slowly as all he could say was, "I… don't… know."

Mr. Owen turned to one of the other troop leaders as if to silently ask for an explanation and could only see a blank look of disbelief. Just as he turned back to the child, hoping to give some reassurance he saw a small, white panel about the size of a cell phone slowly falling like a feather, gently and erratically making its way to the ground and finally coming to rest near little Danny's feet. When Mr. Owen noticed the scorched, jagged edges of the panel he immediately jumped to his feet and surveyed the terrain. Ash had begun filling the air and both large and small pieces of 'something' were beginning to litter the grass with still more in the sky as far upward as one could see.

Chad searched the area for safe cover and saw a large, irregular shaped rock formation that seemed from his vantage point to have a bit of an overhang. *It might just be the perfect place* he thought. "Kids!" he yelled. "Come on! Get to those rocks!" He stood and pointed scanning to make sure every child had heard his instructions. "Hurry! Let's go! Come on!" He continued to scream not knowing how long or how severe this strange event was going to be. One of the other leads was hurriedly guiding the kids while another stood near the entrance to the rock formation waving his arms to help the kids see where they needed to go. Seeing that all the children were on their way, Chad backed off the bolder then scampered down the side of the hill the short distance to the trail then up to meet the others at the formation he was hoping was going to provide enough protection. As the last child safely reached the overhang, Chad took one last look at the scattered dusting of descending debris falling through the air and onto the leaves and branches. He turned to everyone and to no one in particular asked, "What's happening?"

Saturday, February 1, 2003: Nacogdoches, Texas

Stephen F. Austin State University is about 62 miles northeast of Brookeland, Texas, taking about an hour and 15 minutes to drive. But it was a trip that Austin Cole had consistently made three times a week over the last three and a half years, each time barely arriving before his 8:00 a.m. classes. Typically he would try to take a Saturday class because while they were four hours long, they just seemed easier and he could take the full load of semester hours required for his student grant. Saturday classes had always proven to be the most difficult to get up for, though, and make that long drive to Nacogdoches.

Today however, he was feeling pretty good about himself. He had actually gotten up early, had his shower, a piece of toast and some coffee and still had time to do some light studying for the quiz in the Western Civilization class he knew was coming at some point today. He had awakened his step brother, Nick, as he was leaving and was also able to say bye to his dad as he was heading out to class. Austin's step-mother was still asleep, but Nick and his dad were supposed to try to go fishing today, what with the weather expected to be so nice. Austin had come to realize that his dad needed Nick to help fill the void created by him being gone so much. He expected Nick would be needed more after Austin completed college. *Gotta go!* he thought, looking at his watch.

He stopped for a drive-through breakfast on the way in and filled up with gas as he was on about one quarter of a tank and still had to make the drive home after school. Even with all of the delays he managed to reach campus a full half hour before class was to start. The irony of course was that the note on the classroom door when he arrived notified all that class was cancelled today due to the Professor feeling under the weather.

Austin felt both relieved and irritated. He turned to leave the McGee School of Business building, realizing that he now had about an hour's drive home and nothing to do when he got there. All of his friends had already made plans for the day. He decided he'd walk over to the library and spend some time studying before he started back home. On his way out of the building he ran into his classmate Mike Landen, who was on his way to read the same note. Mike's preference was to ditch the library idea and take advantage of the good weather. He and Austin began their stroll over to the AG fountain, sat down in the grass, looked out at the fountain and soaked in the warmth of the sun. At first they began to discuss class issues and the pending test but of course one thing led to another and eventually the subject was girls, then cars, Texas football, and an upcoming social event.

"So, you think you'll try to go to the Delta Tau dance tonight?" asked Mike, already knowing the answer but trying to get Cole out of his pattern of work and school.

"Well, I'm thinking about it," replied Austin half-heartedly. "It's a long drive. I don't get to see my dad that much and I think he's been getting worse." Austin's head lowered a bit. "He doesn't really let us in on how he's feeling but we can kind of sense it. I'll probably just stay around the house. See what I can do for him."

"I figured that's what you'd say but I thought I'd ask," Mike responded. "Besides," taking a bit of a jab, "I'm glad you're not coming. With all those hot girls there I really don't need the extra competition!" Mike grinned as he tapped his friend's shoulder trying to raise his spirits a bit.

Lifting his head, Austin chuckled. "Yeah, like I'd be… any… comp…" The sound of Austin's voice trailed off. His words disappeared. His smile morphed into a confused stare. "Do you see that?" he asked, never taking his eyes from the sky.

Mike's head tilted upward, almost unable to speak. "What the hell?" Then there was just quiet. It even seemed as though there was no sound coming from the water fountain. Both young men looked to the northwest sky intrigued by the trailing light and smoke display spreading across the otherwise cloudless sky never seeming to dispense or dissolve. It just lingered there.

"What the hell is that?" Both spoke at almost precisely the same time.

Saturday, February 1, 2003:
National Weather Service,
Shreveport,Louisiana

At the National Weather Service offices located in Shreveport, Louisiana, the coffee pot was the busiest point in the building. Usually tracking severe weather for the southern region of the U.S. this time of year, there was a fair amount of atmospheric activity to keep everyone busy. However, as the overnight was quiet and the day looked to be more of the same, most of the 11 meteorologists were in groups near or around that morning tradition of coffee and conversation before the work day starts. There are several work stations surrounding the room and four to six down the center that are usually permanently manned. Each station was in turn responsible for smaller areas of the region. On the walls there were several monitors mounted that kept an eye on regional and national radar as well as a few offshore.

Jessica Mitchell had been sitting at her station for about 20 minutes sifting through the pile of data on her desk and occasionally looking up at the three monitors staged side-by-side for easy viewing. Oscar Byrd walked by, cup of coffee in hand, and sat at his station next to Jessica's, offering a hardy "Good morning!" as he placed his cup on his desk.

"Good morning," she replied without really letting her eyes leave the pile of paper in front of her.

"Well, it looks like it's going to be a really good one for somebody," he said wryly.

Jessica turned to see Oscar's gaze leading her to look at the group of co-workers staring at a mounted screen near the far corner of the office area.

"Guess so." She glanced up. "They're all into that

storm heading to the northeast." She reached for her cup, took a sip, and lowering the cup said, "Going to be one of those kind of days."

"Yep," he agreed. "Well, let's see if anything interesting happened last night," Oscar brimmed. Jessica returned to her stack of print-outs as well, taking another sip of coffee and another look over at the monitors, one of which now had a linear pattern developing. It was still undefined but definitely there. She checked another monitor. Changed a setting then changed it back. Looked back to the other monitor, her expression intense and focused.

"Oscar, are you seeing this?" she asked as she pointed to her screen. Oscar raised his head and looked over at her screen but had to lift himself out of his seat just a bit to get a better look. He paused. Turning his head back toward his own screens, he began to see the same bright red, linear pattern beginning to take shape against the black and green background of the screens.

"Well, I see it," he said and paused. His head swiveled from one monitor to the next. "But, I don't know!"

Jessica stood and called for Traci Benton, the office manager who was across the room with the others. "Traci. Can you come and take a look at this?" her bewilderment obvious on her face. "I don't have a clue what this is."

Traci almost casually walked over to Jessica, her

eyes already beginning to steer toward the screen as she got closer. There was silence. She slid in beside Jessica and slowly began to take her seat. She changed some settings then changed them back. She looked up at the wall with one of the mounted monitors which had a different view of the same region.

"What...? That can't be right." Her attention immediately returned to the monitors before her. "Guys! Come here!" she ordered. Several of the others nearby inched their way over as though they were about to see another funny cloud formation shaped like a penis. For each, as they came closer the smile disappeared. The expectation became intense evaluation.

"What is that?"

"Not a clue!"

"Maybe it's a high altitude dust storm of some kind."

Before the next set of questions and answers could be verbalized there came a loud shriek from the break room.

"Oh, my god!" A head peaked around the corner. "Guys, you've got to see this. Hurry!"

Everyone rushed to the break room and immediately their attention was drawn to the television monitor broadcasting CNN's live coverage of the "Landing of STS-107, the Space Shuttle Columbia," only it wasn't going to be landing...

CHAPTER ONE

(11 Years Later)Friday, June 12th, 4:30 a.m.

Quiet and still dark outside, the screeching of the morning alarm brought about an abrupt end to an otherwise peaceful night of sleep. Austin rolled to his right and let his left hand drop on top of the radio to silence its persistent screams, then rolled onto his back for just a few more seconds of rest. Half awake, he lay there contemplating the day ahead and trying to motivate himself to get up and get started. He slowly sat up in his bed, shuffled his hands through his slightly wavy, disheveled brown hair to shake off the cobwebs, and then leaned forward into a standing position. He stumbled to the bathroom door, took a quick pee, turned on the shower to let it warm up, then headed to the kitchen for his morning cup of coffee which he had readied and programmed for brewing before he went to bed the night before.

After filling his cup, he turned and walked the short hallway to Nick's room to wake him so that he too could get ready for work. Nick didn't like the alarm clock and was really quite talented at ignoring it whenever he did set it. Austin was his safety net. Today was no exception. He entered Nick's room.

"Nick!" He said. "Time to get up. Let's go!" He waited a minute just to be sure he too wasn't being ignored. As insurance he asked, "You awake?"

Nick began to stir just a bit and managed a sleepy, "Yes."

Austin thought how much his life had changed over the last seven years. His mother had passed away soon after he started college. Two years later his father re-married and Austin had inherited a step-brother. Nick and Austin had become close over the few years they were together. "Coffee's ready!" called Austin as he headed back to the shower. Both grieved when Nick's mother was killed in a car wreck while Austin was on one of his 'trips' after he graduated from college. *Where was I when that happened?* He couldn't be sure. He didn't get word until after the funeral. He felt really guilty for not being there for Nick. He'd already lost a father at age ten and then he lost his mother. Nick was still very young having just started high school and the loss of his mother was difficult. Austin, when he was home, represented a friend and a stabilizing figure to Nick that Austin's dad couldn't provide.

It was kind of the same situation for Austin. His mother passed when he was a teenager, but that was after a long battle with cancer. When his dad passed, no one really saw it coming except, perhaps, his doctor. Whenever Austin was able to make it back home during those days he could see that his father seemed weaker, less active and engaging but thought it was just due to getting older. The heart attack claimed him seemingly without warning. *Never made it to be old,* Austin thought.

It was the right thing to do, moving back home and taking care of Nick. At least he'd have some sense of stability. The stability was good for Austin, too, but he was still hurting some. He had been enjoying his life but didn't want Nick in a foster home, so he felt he only had one choice. And being able to live in the same house he grew up in made the adjustment easier.

Thirty five minutes later Nick came walking out of the kitchen with a piece of toast in one hand and his gear for work in the other. He passed Austin on his way to the front door.

"You coming?" Nick teased.

"Right behind you little brother." Austin quipped. "Besides, I'm driving so you aren't leaving without me!"

After a twenty minute drive, Austin and Nick arrived in Jasper, Texas, at their current job site, a four story office complex. The first light of the day was just beginning to show itself as they parked the faded, light green, 2002 Ford F150 pickup in the dusty gravel parking lot near the site. They got out of the truck, gathered their gear, locked the truck, and it was time to start work. A June day in Texas never made for a fun day at work when you were in construction. After hearing the day's weather report on the radio on the way in to work, neither were looking forward to the pending 103 degree temperature later in the afternoon.

"Have a good one." Nick said as he walked onto the work site.

"Be safe." Austin replied heading off to the portable offices. As the construction manager for the job he planned, monitored, and managed the day's events. Austin felt really bad for Nick because he was a welder and by late this afternoon, in this heat his body was going to be completely drained. He never seemed to complain much though. It was what he was trained for and what he wanted to do. The good news was that it was Friday and that meant the shift ended after only nine hours! *Good times*.

The day went by as quickly as a Friday could when you're looking forward to a weekend. By the time Austin rounded the corner of the portable offices Nick was already waiting at the truck, his gear loaded in the back. He was sitting on the running board on the driver's side using both hands to hold his head up. Austin came walking up with his hard hat in one hand, a big binder in the other and his truck keys dangling from his right finger.

"I am so ready to go!" Austin's tired words seemed forced as he opened the truck door and placed the binder and hard hat in the back seat.

"Yep," was about all Nick could muster having already walked to the passenger side. "Me too," he said as he climbed inside, flopped into his seat and buckled up.

The twenty minute drive home seemed much longer than usual. The buildup of sweat and grinding dust made both sitting and breathing uncomfortable. Nick was kind of slumped in the seat with his head leaned against the window, while Austin was slouched over the steering wheel as if he were using it to hold himself up. Finally, he leaned back in the seat, gave Nick a gentle slap on the arm as if to make sure he hadn't fallen asleep.

"So, what have you got planned for tonight?" he asked. Nick slid up in the seat a bit and rubbed his hand across his mouth.

"Well, I'm going over to David's. We're going to go get something to eat then maybe go back to his mom's place and play Xbox or something." Nick answered with more enthusiasm than Austin had expected. "What about you?"

"I'm going to meet up with Butch and Randall," replied Austin, as the truck came to a stop in the driveway, "maybe Matt if he can convince his girlfriend to let him out." The doors swung open, and Austin and Nick raced to the house, each slapping the back door to claim victory, before Austin hit the showers and headed to the bar. "We're going to go to Roper's and get some wings, have some drinks, and shoot some pool," Austin announced as he picked up his keys and headed to the door.

Roper's was a little place back in Jasper that was host to live bands, country music, dance, pool, darts and some really great wings. It was most well-known however for the patronage of attractive, available young women. The bar was fortunate enough to be located within walking distance from the hospital located about a block and a half down and across the street. Many of the hospital staff spent some of their after-hours and lunch breaks socializing and eating wings. Most of the staff were women. *The guys love that place!* Austin smiled.

By 8 o'clock pretty much everyone had arrived at the bar and had gotten the night off to a good start by racking up the balls and stacking up the wings. Most of the guys preferred their wings to have a good bite but Austin liked the mild better, so he'd only eat a couple. That was about all he could handle before he had to drink more beer than he should just to cool his mouth off.

Roper's was a fairly casual bar. There were a couple of businessmen at a table that still hadn't taken off their ties or jackets, but for the most part the guys were wearing jeans and a short sleeve Polo or button-up shirt. The women had on jeans or nice slacks and some fairly fancy blouses with the exception of those on lunch break from the hospital who were wearing their scrubs.

Matt was able to join the guys allowing them to have teams to play pool. Each player would alternate taking shots. As usual, when it wasn't their turn to at the table, Butch and Randal took the opportunity to scope out the women present, commenting here and there on how hot that one was or how that one was too tall. Neither really had the courage to actually talk to any of them so it didn't matter. But it was still a fun exercise.

There were a few girls who were regulars on Friday nights. Matt had noticed that Austin may have been interested in one in particular, a pretty brunette about five foot two inches tall, kind of slender but with some curves. She had a pretty face and always seemed to be smiling whenever Austin glanced her way. It was pretty obvious that she was interested as well but neither seemed to want to take the first step and introduce themselves. Austin had started to make the move a couple of times, but one of the guys would always say or do something that would embarrass him before he got started.

By 12:30 a.m. the guys were pretty much done for the night. In fact, Matt had already left the bar as he had promised his girlfriend he'd be home before 11:00. After paying their bar tab and collecting their stuff, they got up and headed for the exit. Butch and Randall were still trying to get Austin to man-up and go talk to the pretty brunette but he would have none of it.

"It's a little too late for that!" exclaimed Austin as he reached for his truck keys. "Besides, Nick's at home alone and I'd better get home and check in on him."

"Oh man!" cried Butch. "That's just an excuse."

Randall chimed in. "Yeah, what a coward!"

Austin just shook his head with a smirk on his face and said "Go home!" He turned to walk away, keys in hand and headed down the sidewalk toward his truck which was parked on the street about a block and a half from the club. Butch and Randall had both parked in the lot across the street so they said their good-byes and went their separate ways.

As he walked along, the ringing in his ears began to subside and he enjoyed the quiet almost deserted city streets except for the cars parked along each side of the street and those parked in the lot. There was not a car in motion or a soul in site with the exception of two guys sitting in a dark-colored, late model sedan which he found a bit strange. *Hmm, wonder if they're gay?* he thought as he turned and stepped off the curb between the front of his truck and the back of the car parked ahead of his.

Just as he started to turn to his left and reach for the door to his truck he heard the sound of a car approaching from his right. It was Butch's 2010, red Mustang. He came driving by, window down and hand hanging out. "Go home you tired old man!" he shouted. Austin just smiled, waved him off, then opened his truck door and started the long drive home.

Twenty minutes later Austin was approaching his driveway, well lit by the power company light across the street from the entrance. He turned on his signal and as he began to slow he noticed that the porch light, which Nick usually left on for him, was not on. *He must have already gone to bed,* he thought. *Little shit! Didn't even leave a light on for me.* He pulled up the driveway and parked his truck just in front of the stand-alone, two-car garage off to the left of the house.

Just before he shut the truck lights off, he saw that the walk-through door to the garage was open. *Boy! He must have really been beat!* he thought as he shut the truck off and walked over to the door, pulled it closed and locked it. Turning back toward the house, he walked down the driveway just a bit to get to the sidewalk and up to the front porch. Just as he reached the stairs to the porch he could clearly see that the both the screen door and front door were left wide open. *Holy Shit!* he thought. *We've been robbed!*

Almost immediately it occurred to him that the robbers may still be inside and his brother may be a hostage. He quickly crouched down and quietly rushed back to the passenger side door of his truck. He unlocked the door, opened the glove compartment and pulled out his 9mm, semi-automatic pistol, checked the clip, loaded the chamber, then turned back toward the house. This time however, he was going in the back way.

CHAPTER TWO

Thursday, June 11th, 10:18 a.m.:
NSA Headquarters, Maryland

Agent Rachael Birch, an analyst with NSA assigned to the Deep Cover Counter Terrorism Unit was monitoring on-line chatter at her station along with twenty-two other agents. Agent Birch is a bright, twenty-eight year old, five foot six inches tall, with sandy-blond hair, green eyes, athletic figure and model–like skin tone. She was recruited directly out of college and after two years of training and working on small projects for Homeland Security, she was transferred to the DCCT unit.

The DCCT unit is currently housed on a fourth floor office building. The DCCT offices have an open floor plan, multiple workstations and each with two desktop LCD monitors. This was not a quiet work environment as almost every agent at a desk was wearing headphones with microphones and talking at breakneck speeds all while typing. Agent Birch was one of the few currently unengaged in phone conversation. At this moment she was busy reading through electronic documents searching for key words and making notations at each appearance in a document. Just as she identified another keyword and was about to make her notation her desk phone rang.

"Are you sure?" she asked firmly and confidently. "What was the time?" She made the notation. "Duration?" she asked, again waiting for the response from the other end of the line. "Look, just give me everything you've got right now!" she demanded. She was quiet for several moments but frantically writing everything down.

"Hold on, please." She moved her computer mouse and made a few clicks. Screens on each monitor were changing rapidly, another click, then another. "Ok, so how long before you can get me the complete transcription?" Again, she wrote. Then she typed. A few more clicks with screen changes and back to the writing.

Birch looked closely at her notes, then quickly back to the monitors where she went through the process again to double check every detail. She felt certain now. She pushed her seat back, stood abruptly, reached down and picked up her hand written notes and turned away. She had the length of what seemed like Grand Central Terminal to walk before she came to the stairs leading to the directors' offices located one level up.

The directors' offices formed a circle around the

open office area, similar to a walking track built inside a gymnasium but one floor level up. The walls to the offices were made of thick, clear glass as were the doors. Birch could see Director Hughes at his desk working through some paperwork. She could tell no one was in the office with him and the headset of his phone was on the receiver. She didn't see his lips moving so she hoped she wasn't disturbing him.

While professionally attired wearing navy blue slacks with a tailored white, button down blouse and form-fitting navy blazer, she walked as though she'd feel much more comfortable in flip-flops than in the matching navy colored three inch heels she was currently wearing. In spite of the struggle she scampered as best she could up the stairway then down the hall to Director Hughes's office. She knocked on the door even though the director could clearly see her approaching. He motioned her in.

"What is it?" asked the director, as Agent Birch approached his desk.

"We have another active contact on OS231, sir."

"Are you sure it's active?"

"Yes, sir," she replied. "Two keywords and one subjective," she explained.

"Do we know the origin yet?"

"We know it's somewhere in East Texas," she replied. "We expect to have a definitive answer in about an hour." She continued, "The call was initiated at 7:22 p.m. and lasted seven minutes, eight seconds."

The director looked directly at Agent Birch. "Was there an NDA breach?"

"I don't think so," she said. "I expect to get the complete transcription in about an hour."

"When you get it, come see me immediately." He reached for his phone, pressed four digits and the speaker came alive.

"Yes, sir."

"Matthews, please come to my office for a moment," the director said, speaking pleasantly but giving a direct order. "Hold on just a minute, Rachael," he said, waiting for Matthews to arrive.

Agent Birch debated whether to sit or continue to stand. She stepped back a bit, just as she saw Matthews in her peripheral coming down the hall. In seconds he had opened the door and stepped inside the director's office. He acknowledged Agent Birch as he moved in toward the desk behind which Director Hughes sat, still looking through the paperwork spread across his desk.

"Hi, Bob," the director said cordially. "Bob, we need to get two field agents briefed and ready to go to Texas." He pointed slightly at Agent Birch. "Rachael is going to be getting a package together for them. We should know within the hour if we're sending them or not."

"Mission parameters, sir?" asked Matthews.

"Well, that all depends on what Agent Birch has for us in about an hour. You get the agents together and we'll all meet back here in about 45 minutes."

No need to be told, both Matthews and Birch turned and exited the director's office, each heading immediately to their respective stations to begin their tasks. Forty-five minutes later Birch's phone rang. "Great!" she responded. "Bring it up immediately." Seven minutes later, Birch was once again walking into Director Hughes's office. Matthews and two field agents were already there.

"Sir, we have the transcript," stated Rachael, her voice a bit flustered. "The second call originated from Brookeland, Texas, on Tuesday, June 9th at 7:22 p.m. The call ended at 7:29 p.m."

Director Hughes interrupted the agent. "Hold on, Rachael. Let's let everyone in on what's going on here."

"Yes, sir." Turning to the two field agents, he said, "We have a long-standing operation of ongoing sur-veillance tagged OS231 that we've been monitoring. Over the past four years there have been no suspicious contacts. That is, until a little over three weeks ago when there was a flagged subject contact and while the sensitive subject involving OS231 did not include a breach of the NDA surveillance of that contact be-gan as well. Then, on Tuesday OS231 received a second subject contact. I have here the transcript of subject contact two." Rachael looked at the director. He nodded as if giving approval to proceed.

"The following is the transcript."

OS231: Hello.

Subject: Hi. My name is Nick Sims. I'm from Brookeland, Texas. Am I speaking with Howard Cromwell?

OS231: Yes. I'm Howard Cromwell. (Pause) What's this about?

Subject: Sir, are you the Howard Cromwell that works at NASA?

OS231: No. I'm retired. I used to work there about seven years ago. Why?

Subject: But you did work there during the Columbia tragedy, right?

OS231: I did. (Pause) What do you want?

Subject: Well sir, I've been studying everything I could find on that mission. I studied it from beginning to end. I've studied the manifest, the crew, mission control, just about anything that I could find and....

OS231: What's this got to do with me?

Subject: Well, like I said, I've done a lot of research but I still have a lot of questions and I was hoping that you could help me.

OS231: Look son, I don't know anything. Besides,

when you work for NASA you sign an NDA that's binding for 50 years so I couldn't talk to you about this even if I wanted to."

Subject: But couldn't you just answer a couple of questions about the missing chamber that no one seems to know about?

OS231: Hangs up.

Call concluded.

Director Hughes looked up at the two field agents. "You two need to be on a plane to Texas in 20 minutes." He looked at Agent Birch, "I want them fully briefed on the subject of OS231. I want them to know what he looks like, who he talks to, who he texts, who he calls. I want his emails, what web pages he visits, what searches he's run."

Agent Birch started to leave. "I'll get right on it, sir."

"Rachael, I want them to have the complete package by the time they land in Houston."

"Yes, sir." Rachael left the office and went straight to her desk and began work.

The director looked back at the two agents who were still patiently waiting for their instructions. "I want to know who subject contact two is, what he knows, how he got OS231's phone number and more importantly, I want to know what connection he has to the contact from three weeks ago." The agents and Matthews turned to leave. "Give me regular updates, Bob. I don't want any surprises."

CHAPTER THREE

Saturday, June 13th, 12:30 a.m.

As Austin moved cautiously toward the back porch, he could see that the security light mounted to the garage, was keeping the porch fairly well lit and could clearly see that this door was wide open as well. It also occurred to him that standing in that doorway would present a perfect target were someone inside, armed and waiting for him. *Damn!* Realizing all the noise he had made as he pulled in the driveway, he just shook his head. *Well, that means they know I'm here, but they may not know where I'm at.* He carefully crawled up the steps and onto the porch. Inching his way closer to the lower of the two windows before him, he realized that he was breathing so quietly that his lower back was beginning to hurt as though he'd held his breathe for too long.

He finally slinked up to the bottom left corner of the window to the dining room. As he lifted his head slightly to enable his right eye to peer inside, he also raised the gun in his right hand ever so slightly, more instinctively than in preparation. His initial peek provided little clarity. He didn't see anyone or any activity in that area of the house but was sure he hadn't seen enough to rule it out. He lowered himself and the gun in his hand back down to the porch floor, wondering on the way down if he'd actually be able to use it to shoot someone. After all, it had been so long since he'd last fired a weapon. *But, Nick may be in there.* Sitting with his back against the house and knees bent, he convinced himself that he could if he had to. Then, determined to take another, longer look, he turned and raised himself again but this time turning his head so that both eyes could get more detail.

He had gotten his bearing and this time he could see that the room was empty except for the table and chairs. The lower doors to his mother's china cabinet were open and everything inside was strewn all over the floor. Otherwise everything appeared intact. Now it was time to move down the porch and over to the kitchen window. He didn't want to cross in front of the door which led into the kitchen so he again crawled down off the porch and over to the side nearest the kitchen window.

He knew this was going to be more dangerous as the window he had to look through was higher off the porch than the other at the dining room. It was over the sink, meaning he'd be more exposed as he glanced inside. He'd again have to make this quick but, because of the angle of the window and the porch roof to the security light on the garage, he also knew it would be easier to see inside. *What a break,* he thought, knowing this would be the room he would have to enter. *Or was it?*

He leveraged himself up to the window, using his feet to push his back against the outside wall of the house and just to the left of the window. This time he brought the pistol with him realizing that it was almost pointed at his chin. He moved the firearm away slightly as he slowly leaned around the window frame then retracted. *Looks clear.* He leaned again, this time taking a long look. All of the doors on the kitchen cabinets were open but it didn't look as though anything had been taken out. He assumed the cabinet doors under the sink were open as well.

He spun across to the other side of the window realizing that he was now closer to the doorway but he needed to get a better view of the pantry. *Like everything else,* he thought. *Door open!* He did notice something on the floor in front of the pantry door but couldn't make it out. *Looks like the trash can.* He turned, gun raised chest high and close to his body just like he'd seen on those television shows. *Alright, time to go in.*

He stayed low as he entered the room well aware of the doorway to the dining room and then to the rest of the house. He scanned the kitchen one more time, finding nothing but open doors and things in general disarray. Next he focused entirely on the entrance to the dining room. He took a short step to his right to get a glimpse of the hallway which led from the dining room past the bathroom and into the living room. *Not enough light!* He stepped around the island that was located in the center of the kitchen and stooped down near the end, taking aim at the access to the dining room not seven feet away.

He decided it was time to make his move into the dining room. Staying low, he scooted around the end of the island then darted to the wall on the right side of the doorway. The 9mm was pointed directly down the hallway as he took several snapshot looks for any movement down the dark hall. *Someone could be in the bath,* he thought, knowing that it was well hidden between the dining room and living room at the front of the house.

As he started down the hallway he kept his left shoulder and back in contact with the left wall allowing him the best view of the bathroom entrance. With each step both the interior of the bathroom and the expanse of the living room became more visible with no noticeable target. He sprung into the bathroom and turned the gun quickly toward the shower then breathed a quiet sigh of relief to find it empty.

As he started out of the bathroom he noted the staircase leading to the upstairs from the front of the living room. He knew if he got too far into the open in the living room someone may have a clear shot from the top of the stairs, so he stooped down and went back against the stairway wall to confirm the living room was clear. He turned to place his right shoulder against the wall, gun raised towards the top of the stairs, which was difficult to see as there was a landing about one third of the way up. He started inching his way backward until he reached a clear line of sight to the top, checking the front door to his back occasionally just to be safe.

Before he started up the stairs he turned to the master bedroom that was across from the living room. *Ok, problem here is two closets,* he thought. *Really good place to hide.* He looked right then left. Both doors to the closets were open and most of the clothes strewn on the bed or floor. Anything non-clothing was also taken out of the closets and obviously, just thrown to the floor. The bed, too, had been moved as if someone had checked both under the bed itself and between the mattresses.

Feeling confident now that the bottom floor of the house was secure, it was time to address the second floor which consisted of two bedrooms separated by a shared bathroom. As he peered up the dark stairs it was clear there wasn't enough light to safely make it to the top so he turned to his left and opened the top drawer of one of the end tables nearest to where the sofa once sat upright, then pulled out a flash light. With the light in his left hand, the gun firmly in his right, and both pointed directly up the stairs, he took his first step. Three steps later he was at the landing, stooped and pointing the flashlight, when he realized the flashlight only made it easier for anyone hidden upstairs to target him. *Let's make it fair,* he thought, when he saw the light switch for the staircase and upstairs hallway. He flipped the switch and started his ascent.

Once he reached the top floor he could easily see inside the upstairs bath. The curtain was already open and empty. He turned his attention to bedrooms on either side of the bath, not really sure which to check first. Austin looked at Nick's room and decided it would be the easiest to inspect because his room was arranged with the closet directly across from the bedroom entrance so he could clearly see it from where he was standing. Empty. Every bit of clothing strewn on the floor or bed, shoes out, boxes and containers dumped and dropped.

Austin twisted to his right to get a look at the back of the room, took an over the shoulder glance back toward the other bedroom before he decided to enter this one. Gun raised, he stepped inside the doorway and scoped the rest of the room. The room was in shambles but no one inside.

The last bedroom to search was his own. He knew it well as he'd grown up there, having never had the heart to move downstairs into his father's bedroom once he passed away. That's where it felt like home. He inched his way back down the narrow hallway to the door and using his left hand reached inside, to the left of the door frame and flipped on the light switch. Again, the room was trashed but no one present. *I guess they're gone,* he thought, lowering his weapon, turning to go over to the night stand next to his bed. He slowly sat down and reached over to the phone located just next to the alarm clock and dialed the police.

Knowing it would take at least 15 minutes for an officer to arrive, Austin decided to search the garage as he had remembered the walk-through door to it was open when he arrived and, while he doubted it, there might still be someone in there. *I at least need to know what it looks like in there.* He thought about all of his tools and some of his dad's things that he had stored in there that a thief might find of value. With a sigh, he picked up his handgun, stood to his feet and worked his way back outside to the back porch.

As he stood at the edge of the porch he was fully drenched in light since he'd turned on every lamp and light in the house on his way out, including those outside that he could turn on from inside. Unfortunately, there was no switch inside the house to turn on the lights in the garage. The only real light he had to work with was falling from the security lamp on the garage roof. While he now believed he was alone, he stealthily moved to the side of the garage keeping out of sight of the windows and avoiding the garage door. With gun raised, he stood at the front right corner of the garage, glanced around the corner, stooped down and began to slide his way past the first large garage door, coming to a stop at the edge of the walk through.

Reaching across his squatting body with his left hand he gently pushed the door. It didn't budge. *Damn.* Remembering he'd closed and locked it when he first got home. *How do I unlock it without setting myself up?* He fumbled through his pockets to see if he still had his keys, not able to remember if, in all the excitement, he may have laid them down in the kitchen or living room. *Great!* He pulled them out and shuffled through them until he found the needed key.

He knew that in order to open the door he was going to have to be on the other side, adjacent to the left side garage door. He suddenly spun 180 degrees resting his left shoulder against the door frame. With the key in his left hand he was able to insert and turn the key to open the door without reaching in front of it. The lock released. He turned the knob and gently pushed on the door so that it would only open a few inches. *Don't want to give anyone a clear shot.* He paused.

The light switch was just inside the door to the left and the door opened inward and to the right. He didn't need much of an opening to reach his arm through in order to locate and flip the switch. However, he'd have to use his right hand, meaning he'd have to move the gun to his left. He was naturally right handed and had never fired a weapon left handed before. He had no choice. He slowly reached in and flipped the switch.

With the lights now on it was clear, while trashed, the thieves were gone. Austin stepped inside and began to look through the mess scattered around the garage. Some things were broken as a result of being thrown but most everything was still there and in pretty good shape. He first located the storage containers with mementos of his dad's he'd stored away. Almost all were opened, dumped out and boxes thrown off to one side or the other. His nervousness had been replaced with anger, just as the BCPD cruiser pulled into his driveway.

CHAPTER FOUR

Friday, June 12th, 11:22 a.m.:
New York City, New York

K ao Yi Fun entered the United States on a Japanese passport under the name of Wu Yin, an elementary school teacher from Tokyo. In fact, when asked by the customs agent upon arrival for the purpose of her visit, Yi Fun answered quite honestly, "I am here to visit my brother. He is a student at MIT." The customs agent carefully evaluated her facial expressions as she made her statement. He then compared the passport photo to the face before him. He scanned the coded passport, waited for any warnings to pop up, then stamped her arrival, and just like that Agent Kao Yi Fun of China's Ministry of State Security was on American soil.

After leaving the customs area of J.F.K. International Airport, Yi Fun picked up her luggage, took the tram to the nearest train station and purchased her ticket to Cambridge, Massachusetts. She boarded the train eight minutes later, found a place for her luggage, then sat alone for the four hour trip that would require at least two train changes ultimately ending with a 30 minute MBTA trip to Lechmere Station.

On the next-to-last leg of her train ride she decided to use the time to revisit the facts as she already knew them and prepare for her approach upon arriving at her brother's rented apartment near the campus of the Massachusetts Institute of Technology. Her brother was supposedly renting an apartment near a place called Hurley Park on Hurley Street and Fifth Avenue. She estimated a 10 minute cab ride from the hotel if it was needed. She'd have the cab from the train station drive by that hotel on his way to her brother's apartment. *Should not be that far out of the way,* she thought.

She and her brother, Yi Szun, were both born in a comparatively small town northwest of Shanghai, China, in the province of Jiangsu, called Nanjing. Their family was fortunate to have been allowed to have a second child, an opportunity almost 40 percent of the coastal population in China is not afforded. Both children were well educated and graduated from their respective high schools with honors which allowed them the good fortune to attend university.

Yi Fun, an attractive, intelligent and athletic young woman of five foot five inches tall, was recruited during her last year of college to join the MSS. She was, in fact, already in training upon her successful completion of school. After four and a half years of training and active service she was considered one of the top active field agents in service of the MSS. She wondered briefly if that would continue to be the case upon her return.

Her brother pursued a much different path. While not as athletic as his sister, he was more talented in the classroom. His particular interests were physics and mathematics at which he excelled. Upon his graduation from college, he was presented with a scholarship opportunity to complete a Master's Degree in Particle Physics at MIT, an opportunity Yi Fun often thought may have been motivated more by state interests than by recognition of potential by an outside entity. After all, having the brother of one of your finest agents in the United States on a student visa had to present a great deal of opportunity for the advancement of state priorities.

The Amtrak train started to slow as it streaked through a small Massachusetts town. Yi Fun decided this was the time to get her papers together. She stood up and pulled her smallest bag from the shelf above her seat, dug around, and found the button to open the hidden compartment which popped with the sound of a spring recoiling. She reached into the compartment and pulled out several passports, a small stack of cash and an American driver's license. She shrewdly placed the cash and the license in the seat next to her hip, closest to the window. She thumbed through the passports and found the one with her last name, same as the license, but which identified her as a Canadian resident.

While back in Shanghai preparing for this trip, she

knew in order to access any of her brother's records she would have to have a plausible identity. She constructed passports and driver's licenses, several credit cards and other papers that would identify her as Kao Li Yin. This would enable her to introduce herself as the sister of Kao Yi Szun.

As she departed the Harvard Square train station, she pulled her luggage behind with one hand and her purse in the other, looking every bit the part of an out-of-towner not sure where she's going. She located the appropriate MBTA train that would take her on to Lechmere Station. Again, she secured her luggage but without the benefit of the overhead shelf. She kept most of it at her feet or within arm's length as the car was crowded with rush-hour travelers on their way home.

Upon arrival at Lechmere Station, she gathered luggage, disembarked from the train, worked her way through the station then finally stepped out onto the sidewalk. Outside there were taxi-cabs lined up to take new arrivals to their destination and the next in line pulled forward to the loading lane as Yi Fun approached the curb. The driver popped the trunk from the inside, then walked around to help load the luggage.

Seconds later they departed for Hurley Street and ultimately her brother's apartment. Just as she had planned, the driver took the route she requested so that she could evaluate the Hotel Marlowe. Her hope, of course, was that she would find her brother safely at home, with an understandable reason for not calling and thereby be glad to see her and encourage her to stay with him during her short visit. In the event that it was necessary to have lodging for the night, this hotel was close enough that Yi Fun could be at the apartment quickly if needed.

The cab pulled up to the apartment at the address provided by Yi Fun and came to a halt. The driver was asked by Yi Fun to stay briefly as she may need further service if her brother was not home. She walked up one flight of stairs and arrived at apartment 3, knocked on the door and waited. After what she felt was an appropriate amount of time she knocked again but still no response. She took a quick look at the doorknob and lock. The deadbolt was set. *That may make things more difficult,* she thought as she weighed her options.

Yi Fun walked across the hallway to apartment #4 and knocked on that door hoping to speak to a neighbor. A few moments later the door opened and a young woman, tall with sandy-blonde hair and a pretty face appeared and said, "Yes?"

"Hello," Yi Fun began. "My name is Kao LiYin." She turned with a slight motion toward the door across the hall. "My brother lives in Apartment 3. I knocked but there was no answer. I've tried calling several times but again no answer. Do you know where he may be?"

"No," she was quick to reply. "I haven't seen him in weeks. We usually meet every day at the mail boxes down stairs but he hasn't been picking up his mail." She motioned down the stairs. "I think they ended up taking all of it to the manager's office."

"Where might I find this office?" asked Yi Fun.

"It's in the next building down," she said, pointing to some imaginary point in the air to represent the direction down Hurley Street. "The office is on the first floor. You can't miss it as you walk up to the building."

Yi Fun thanked her for her time and returned to the cab. "I will need you to take me to the hotel we passed," she said, leaning in through the passenger side window. "But first, I need to walk up to the manager's office and get some information. It should only take a few minutes."

"That's ok with me, sweetheart. I'm keeping the meter running." The driver pointed to the counter on his dash. "You take whatever time you need."

She nodded her understanding then began walking to the next building. The helpful young woman was correct. The manager's office was clearly identified both near the walkway to the office and on the office door. She knocked on the door. A voice from the other side called "Come on in! It's open!"

Yi Fun opened the door and entered the office where a woman who appeared to be in her middle forties was stepping around her desk about 10 paces from Yi Fun who greeted her with a hearty "Hello."

"Hi. How can I help you?" asked the manager.

"My brother, Kao Yi Szun lives in Apartment 3 and I am told that he has not been home for several weeks." She paused. "Are you aware of where he may have gone?"

"I really have no idea. I do know that he owes me for this month's rent." She reached out for Yi Fun's hand. "I'm sorry. I'm Cindy, the complex manager." She explained that she had checked on a number of occasions, both day and night, to get in touch with him but there was never an answer at the door.

"I understand that you may have his mail," said Yi Fun thinking there may be a clue in that.

"I do," she replied, "but by law, I'm not allowed to give it to anyone but him. I'm sorry."

Yi Fun countered, "May I just look at the mail? There may be something there that may help me find him."

The manager thought carefully for a moment. "Sure." She turned, walked to a different desk, opened the bottom, right side drawer and pulled out a stack of envelopes. Handing them to Yi Fun she said, "Here. Hope this helps."

Yi Fun toggled through the stack, slowly and carefully evaluating every addressee then set them aside.

Toward the bottom of the stack she froze. The addressee on this letter was in fact her brother. The letter was marked RETURN TO SENDER. Yi Fun made note of the address to where the letter was originally sent. *Why would he send mail to Texas?* she wondered. She continued looking through the pile of mail with nothing else of interest getting her attention. Mostly there were offers for credit, a utilities statement, and a bill for cable. Otherwise nothing of interest or anything that she felt she would need to pursue.

She reached for her purse. "How much is my brother's rent?"

"It's 800 dollars," Cindy quickly replied, then added, "but you really don't have to do that. I'm sure he'll be in any time now and take care of it."

"Just to be sure, I will pay." She counted out the 800 US dollars and handed it to the manager. "He can pay me back when he returns." She took the receipt from the manager, thanked her for her help and returned to the cab. It was clear she would need to pay her brother's apartment another visit.

Much later that evening Yi Fun had a taxi drop her off a couple of blocks away and one block down from the apartment building her brother rented. A few short minutes later she was already at the rear of the building. *The poor lighting will be of benefit,* she thought. She stealthily made her way to the rear of the apartment, ducking into shadows and hiding behind an assortment of trash cans or grills. She saw the sliding glass doorway on the deck of her brother's second floor apartment. *Perfect.*

She climbed one of the four inch square, wooden posts which supported the structure and quickly jumped over the railing, immediately ducking down to avoid being seen. She looked through the cracks in the railing. No one seemed to have noticed so she turned her attention to the door. *Good. No security system. This should not be difficult.* She took out a small tool pouch and went to work making short order of opening the door and gaining access.

She quietly walked through the apartment. It was clean, orderly and she noted that it even smelled nice. It also struck her as interesting that the television and peripherals were still in place. She went to the bedroom. The closet door was open but otherwise everything was in its place. Everything that is except for two pieces of the 3 case set of luggage she had purchased for her brother for his trip to the United States. She looked around the room. The largest case was not to be found. She went through his closet and drawers. *Clearly some of his clothing is not here.* Taking one more look around the bedroom then on to the bathroom. Toothpaste, brush and other bathroom sundries all gone.

She walked back into the living area and over to

the small desk next to the gaming station. There were speakers, a printer and a monitor. *Hmm. No computer! He must use his lap top and no tower.* It was clear that Yi Szun had chosen to leave and expected to return soon or he was taken and did not know how long he would be gone. Either way, she knew he was in trouble and the only clue she had was an address in Texas.

CHAPTER FIVE

Saturday, June 13th, 2:10 a.m.: Brookeland, Texas

Leaving the headlamps on, the officer opened his door and stepped out of the car. Austin, who had been leaning against the doorway of the garage, stood upright and went to meet him. "Hey!" he said, his tone somewhat dejected. "Sorry to get you out at this time of the night."

"No problem," the officer's eyes casually combed the area. "Goes with the job." With the addition of the cruiser headlamps the entire area was now flooded with light. "So, sounds like you had some visitors?" He eased his way closer to Austin.

"Yes, sir." Austin stretched out his right hand toward the policeman. "Austin Cole," he introduced himself.

"Craig Jefferies," the officer reciprocated. "Do you have some identification?" His hands went to his hips as Austin reached to his right back pocket and pulled out his wallet, took out his driver's license and handed it to the officer. Jefferies took a close look at the card. "Alright. Well, we're going to need to file a report." Keeping the license he turned. "Let me get my pad."

Officer Jefferies went to the passenger side of his vehicle, opened the door and ducked inside, pulling himself out a few seconds later with a large combination clipboard and pad. He went back to the garage to start collecting the details for his report. "Let me just fill in everything I need from your license." He began writing. Once completed he handed Austin's license back to him and began the interrogation.

"So, Mr. Cole, what time did you arrive home?" The officer wrote as he waited for Austin's reply.

Thinking for a moment, Austin responded, "I got here around 1 o'clock. I had been at Roper's in Jasper with some friends."

The officer looked at his watch. It was now 2:10 a.m. "Any reason you waited so long to call us?" he asked.

"I have a little brother that lives here with me," he explained. "I thought he might be inside, hurt or something."

The officer nodded, "So, is anything missing?" He slowly swung his arm in a sweeping motion all around the area.

"Right now," Austin took a breath and exhaled, "I honestly couldn't tell you." He opened both arms and fanned them toward the house and garage. "Everything is such a mess. Things are just thrown everywhere." Austin stepped toward the house. "Come on. I'll show you".

Jefferies followed Austin to the house, stepping cautiously after initially crossing through the threshold of the back door. He was given a complete tour of the home, every room, taking notes for the entire trip. All the while, Austin was telling him how he entered the house looking for his brother.

Standing in Nick's room, Officer Jefferies asked, "Can you tell if anything of your brother's is missing?"

"Well," Austin surveyed the room. His expression morphed from one of evaluation to growing concern. "My brother!" His pulse rushed! "He's supposed to be here! It's Friday night. He's always home by 11:00 on Fridays!"

"Do you know where he was going tonight, or what he had planned?"

"He said he was going over to his friend's house," Austin replied. "Actually, his friend's mom's house," he said, just to be more accurate. "He always does that on Friday nights after work. They play video games or something." The feeling of concern had grown to desperation. "But he *never* stays out past 11:00 on Fridays!"

"So, what time do you usually get home on Friday night?" Jefferies asked, his eyes still on the pad.

Austin knew where this was going and reluctantly replied, "About 1:00."

"So, how would you know what time he actually gets home?" Jefferies said, just trying to bring some perspective and trying to keep Cole calm.

"I see," the realization of what Jefferies had done now obvious on Cole's face. "Well," he regrouped, "all I know is that every Friday for the last year and a half, he's been in bed sound asleep when I get home".

"Which is around 1:00?" It was a question which sounded more like someone trying to make a point. "So," the officer continued, "how far is his friend's mother's house from here?"

"It's about 15 to 20 minutes," Austin replied.

"Is your brother old enough to drive?"

"Yes," Austin answered, "but he doesn't have a car right now. He just can't afford it yet. He just got his first job out of technical school."

Officer Jefferies thought for a moment. "Any chance he just stayed overnight with his friend?"

Austin thought this one through for a moment. "There's a chance. But he hasn't done that since they were kids. Since high school," Austin continued, "they've gone camping overnight a number of times, but never stayed over at his house."

"Think they went camping tonight and just didn't tell you? Kind of a last minute thing?"

His mind scanned the garage and Nick's room trying to recall. "I don't think so. Nick's camping gear is still in the garage on the floor and his sleeping bag was in his room."

"Do you have his friend's name and address?" Jefferies followed with, "Maybe we can check in with them later today some time."

Austin gave the officer everything he knew about Nick's friend, David. *That pad has to be full by now!* Austin thought. Just at that moment officer Jefferies flipped the pad closed, placed his pen in his shirt pocket and looked up at Austin.

"Well, I have everything I need for now." This time Jefferies placed his hand in front of him which Austin instinctively reached for. "I'll file this report and start asking around." He reached in his other pocket and pulled out a card and handed it to Austin. "Here's my card if you need to get in touch with me."

"Thanks, officer." Austin looked at the card and placed it in his pants pocket.

"I wouldn't worry too much right now. I'm sure you'll find your brother at his friend's house," the officer said, trying to be reassuring. Having made his way back to the cruiser, he turned back to Austin and added, "If you find that something is missing or if anything else comes to mind, drop by headquarters. In any case, we should have a report ready for you by Tuesday that you can file with your insurance company."

Austin immediately understood. *This is cop-speak for 'we're really not going to do anything on this.' Clearly, I'll be doing something!*

By now it was nearly 3:30 a.m. If officer Jefferies was right and Nick had spent the night at David's it would probably scare the hell out of them if he called and woke them at this time of the night. Austin decided to try to straighten some things up in his bedroom and then try to get a few hours of sleep. *Tomorrow is going to be a hell of a day,* Austin thought as he walked around the house and locked all the doors and windows. He turned out a few of the lights but felt better leaving more on than usual. He put the mattress and box springs back on the bed frame, threw some sheets and covers over it, then placed his pillow on top.

Feeling emotionally tired and physically exhausted he laid his head on his pillow. His mind began to fog as he tried to replay the night. His thoughts became convoluted and disjointed as he began to drift off to sleep. *Too sleepy to continue. I'll call Jerry tomorrow.* His body went limp. *He'll know what to do.*

CHAPTER SIX

Saturday, June 13th, 10:30 a.m.:
Brookeland, Texas

The bright morning sunlight fell across the side of the two story home, rushing in through the curtained windows of Austin's bedroom and caught him full on the face. The warmth enhanced by the window enticed him to awaken from his slumber. As he lay there wiping the sleep from his eyes, he glanced over at his nightstand. *What the...?* It was already 10:30 a.m. He was hoping to be awake by 8:00. Apparently, the events of the night before took a bigger toll than he thought. He rolled to a sitting position, took a calming breath and reached for the phone, started to dial then realized he didn't know Jerry's number. He got up and went to get his cell phone which, as he discovered, he'd forgotten to charge. *Maybe there's just enough.* He searched for Jerry's cell number. *Yes!* He started dialing his home phone, and while he was waiting for an answer he plugged his cell in to charge. He waited anxiously.

"Hey, Austin, what's up?" answered Jerry's voice at the other end.

Austin didn't waste time. "Nick is missing."

"What?" Jerry asked. "What happened?"

"I got home last night after staying out with the guys for a while," he started explaining, trying to remain calm, "and the place was a mess. All the lights were off. All the doors open. The whole place just trashed." Austin waited for Jerry to take it in.

"Did you call the police?"

"Sure," he said, making no effort to hide his frustration. "But they're not going to do anything. They just think some punks broke in, couldn't find what they were looking for and left."

"What about Nick?"

"They think that he stayed at his friend David's house last night and didn't bother letting me know." His frustration was growing. "I don't have David's phone number. I know where he lives though. I was planning to head over there in a little while. Would be a big help if you could come with me." Austin thought he sounded like he was begging. Maybe he was.

Jerry's reply was immediate. "No problem. I'll be there in about 20 minutes. I'll have to stop for gas." Jerry Hayes was a Deputy Sheriff for Jasper County, Texas, and had been friends with Austin since high school. They didn't get to spend as much time together just hanging out as they'd like but they still met up for drinks every couple of weekends or maybe a phone call or two just to stay in touch.

The Deputy Sheriff's cruiser pulled into Austin's driveway just as Jerry had estimated. As he got out of the car and braced one arm on the door and the other on top of the car, Austin noted that Jerry was in full uniform, which he found surprising, as typically he had the weekends off. *Doesn't matter,* thought Austin. *He's here.* Austin was ready to go. He dashed off the front porch and down the sidewalk to the cruiser. Jerry never left the driver's side door. As Austin approached the car and opened the passenger side, both he and Jerry slid into their seats and seconds later they were off.

"Didn't expect the full treatment," Austin said questioningly, nodding toward Jerry's uniform.

"I thought it may come in handy." A sly smile formed at the corner of Jerry's mouth. "So, tell me everything."

Austin told him the whole story. He included every detail that he could think of. He described the contents of the house as he'd found them. How he searched every room and then the garage. By the time he got to the part that the policeman seemed convinced that Nick was staying over at David's house, the cruiser was pulling into David's driveway.

As Jerry turned off the motor to the cruiser they saw David in the back yard wearing only shorts, socks and tennis shoes, pushing an old self-propelled mower which apparently no longer self-propelled. David was hot, with sweat beading on his forehead and rolling down his fair skinned chest which was now taking on a reddish tinge. *That won't be good later,* thought Austin. David seemed almost relieved when he noticed Jerry and Austin walking up the driveway and into the back yard toward him. David let the mower motor die, smiled, and waved and went to meet them.

That was the way David was. His personality was contagious. He was almost always smiling and never seemed to meet a stranger. Everyone liked him. Austin always thought of him as being like one of those guys in the movies that always seemed to 'know a guy.' If you needed help with something or needed something done or fixed, David could hook you up. Everybody was David's friend. And David was Nick's friend.

"Hey, Austin," David said, reaching for Austin's hand, and pulling him in for a quick hug as well. He pulled away and looked at Jerry, his expression not quite as relaxed. "Deputy," he said as he nodded in his direction. "So, what's going on?"

Austin spoke first. "Is Nick here?"

David looked a bit puzzled. "No. I took him home about 10:00 last night. He said he was bushed." Trying to be clear, he added, "I guess he'd had a tough day at work."

"Was everything ok with the house when you

dropped him off?" Deputy Owen inquired.

"What do you mean?"

"The lights all working? Doors closed? Anything unusual that you may have noticed while you were there or as you were leaving?"

David thought for a moment but really couldn't focus on what condition the house was in because he had a more pressing question of his own. "What's wrong? What's happened?"

Austin stepped forward slightly as if to comfort David and brace him for what was about to come. "We can't find him," he said softly but directly. "I got home last night, all the lights were off, the doors open, the house was in shambles and Nick was nowhere to be found."

David seemed to stagger a bit, his brow cringing. His eyes began to search wildly as if looking for something specific while at the same time nothing at all. To Austin, it didn't seem like David was breathing. "You ok?"

"Do you have any idea where he may have gone?" asked Jerry, trying to get him refocused.

David started to settle himself. "No. He said he was bushed!" David stated again with more emphasis, feeling both scared and angry.

"David," said Austin. "We're not accusing you of anything. We just need your help to try to figure this out." He put his hand on his shoulder. "Look, as far as we can tell you are his best friend and you were the last one to see him."

There was an awkward silence for what seemed like forever. Then a glimmer appeared in David's eyes as if he'd remembered something. He began to speak. "Look, every Friday Nick comes over and we share our research and then play X-box. We don't usually go out anywhere unless it's to eat or to the library. Once we're done, I drive him home. That's what we do."

"Did anything seem out of the ordinary last night?" Deputy Hayes was looking for some shred or tidbit of information that could help. "Like someone following you or maybe you saw something that didn't seem like a big deal at the time but now seems a bit strange?"

David started to answer, "No. All we did was go to King's and get some burgers and fries and....."

Austin interrupted. "Wait, what research? You said you shared your research. Research on what?"

While in high school David and Nick had formed a bond as result of their common interest in space, space exploration and anything to do with it. When Columbia had been destroyed, their interest had only grown. "We just liked to keep track of it to see if any-more of the debris was found," David explained. "I would go to the library to search for new reports and use their computer because I don't have one," David continued, "then on Fridays we'd meet here and kind of compare notes. When we were done we'd play video games for a while."

"So, what kind of debris were you hoping to find," asked Jerry. "I mean, everything burned up."

"Not really," David responded with increased excitement. "Most people don't know this but there was one experiment found that was completely intact. A bunch of worms or something still in the biological research canisters."

"Have they found anything else since then?" Austin asked.

"Well, it's not so much what they have found that Nick and I were curious about," David replied. "It was the 40,000 pieces of debris that they couldn't identify. Do you think something we found in those files got Nick in trouble?" A thought that had not occurred to either Austin or Jerry.

"Everything ok, David?" David's mother asked, straddling the threshold of the back door and pushing the screen door as wide as her arm would reach.

"Yes, Mom," David called back. Deciding not to worry his mother he thought it a good idea to take this inside. "I've got all my files inside if you think they'll help," David offered. "Come on in." David started toward the house. "I need some lemonade anyway."

Austin and Jerry looked at each other and silently agreed to follow David, doubting that anything in the folder about an accident from 15 years earlier was really going to help them find Nick. *He's just trying to help.* As David pulled ahead Austin leaned over to Jerry. "If it makes him feel better, like he's doing something to help, we might as well." Jerry nodded in agreement and took the two steps up to the porch and into the house.

The smell of freshly cut grass was replaced with what Austin could only conclude was home-made apple pie. *Or, it could be a candle,* he thought. They found their way to a little kitchen table with one chair at each end. David offered them a seat and some lemonade while he went to get his files. His mom got the glasses from the cupboard, placed them on the counter by the sink and filled each to the brim. Making small talk she set a glass on the table in front of Austin and Jerry then turned to repeat the process for David who was walking back into the cramped kitchen with several large, brown folders bulging under his arm. The stack was so big in fact that he had to use his other hand to help control it and keep it from spilling as he walked.

"This is all I've got," David said as he used both hands to place the folders on the table next to the glass of lemonade in front of Austin. "Maybe it'll help."

Austin glanced across the table at Jerry who was subtly attempting to hide his cynical smile from David and his mother. "Thanks, David. Are you sure it's ok to take this?" he asked, half hoping that David's reply would provide him with a good excuse not to.

"No. It's ok," David reassured. "I just hope it helps."

Jerry raised his eyebrows and gave his head a slight tilt as if to say "what can you do" and slid his chair away from the table. He reached down and finished off the lemonade. Austin did the same and stepped toward David.

"Let me know if there's anything I can do to help," David pleaded as he gave Austin another hug.

"You've already been a big help!" *Ok, I lied.* Austin thought. He turned to pick up that tall stack of papers lying on the table, secured them under his arm and turned to leave. "Thanks for the lemonade, Mrs. Maddox. It was good to see you again."

Jerry followed Austin. "Thanks, ma'am. It was really good."

As they sat in the cruiser, seat belts fastened, Austin could see the hint of a smile on Jerry's face. "What are you smiling about?"

"Well," he tipped his head quickly toward the pile of paper in Austin's lap. "Looks like you've got some reading to do." Austin looked at the papers then looked up and out through the front window at the garage, reluctantly acknowledging the seventh circle of boredom hell that was about to come.

CHAPTER SEVEN

Saturday, June 13th, 2:48 p.m.:
Brookeland, Texas

Officer Hayes thought that a visit to King's Hamburgers might give them a lead so they took the five minute drive. He figured by now the shift manager would be in and with a little luck may be the same one that worked the evening shift last night. King's was a family owned diner/fast food restaurant that didn't have a drive-through but did have a walk-up window for those who wanted to order and go. There was also a seating area inside for those who wanted to dine in.

By the time Austin and Jerry pulled into the parking lot of King's it was almost 3:00 p.m. The parking lot for the most part was empty, maybe six vehicles, some of which Jerry was sure belonged to some of the employees. It was a pretty fair assumption as the parking area really consisted of one paved section and then another area that was all gravel. The gravel lot was furthest from the restaurant and it was currently hosting four of the parked vehicles.

"I guess we got here at a good time," Jerry pointed out. "They're not too busy."

Austin had already unbuckled his seat belt before Jerry had the car in park and was already stepping out onto the pavement. Jerry caught up quickly and they made their way to the entrance to the restaurant which was really two entrances, the first a small foyer to get customers out of the weather and second leading directly to the seating area.

As they opened the second door they were met by Rhonda Cook who, as luck would have it, was the second shift manager and just who they needed to talk with. There was an older couple sitting to their left near the side window which faced the paved section of the parking lot. There was another couple with two small children sitting three tables away and against the wall. Jerry estimated the kids were between five and eight years of age. The rest of the tables were empty.

"Hey, guys," called Ms. Cook as she picked up two menus. "Sit where ever you'd like."

Officer Hayes cut her off. "We're not here for a meal." She turned to face them with a concerned expression on her face. "We were hoping we could ask you a few questions about a couple of young men you may have served here last night."

"Sure," she replied, confused.

"Were you working last night between 6:00 and 8:00 p.m.?"

"Yes, sir."

Austin pulled out a picture of his brother and held it up for the manager to see while Jerry asked, "Do you remember seeing this young man, maybe with someone else?"

"No. But I've seen them before." She continued, "They're regulars on Friday nights." She turned and put the menus back on the stack next to the register. "Him and another boy, blondish hair." She held her hand up about two feet above her head. "He was about this tall. Seem like good kids though. They in some kind of trouble?"

"We hope not," Jerry stated quickly. "We can't find this boy," pointing at the photo of Nick that Austin was still holding. "We talked to the other young man and he said they came by here last night," sounding like both a question and a statement. "Are you sure you didn't see them?"

"I'm sure," she stated matter-of-factly. "But I worked the dining room all night and Fridays are crazy busy," she added. "I know they didn't come in here last night," she continued, "but there are a lot of times they just come by the window and take it with them."

"So, did you notice anything out of the ordinary last night while you were working?"

"Not really." Her head had turned slightly as she noticed another older couple coming in through the first door. "Sorry I couldn't be more help."

Jerry and Austin thanked her for her time, turned and left. As they stepped out into the parking lot, Austin said, "Well, that was a waste."

"Not really." Jerry clarified, "We just know that since they didn't eat inside there wasn't really anything anyone would have seen." Jerry looked at his watch. "We may have time to swing by the library before they close just in case Nick went there for some reason."

A few minutes later they arrived at the library but the doors were already locked and there was no sign of Nick in the area. They figured he had to be walking since his bike was still in the garage at Austin's house. With no other lead to follow, Jerry decided to take Austin home and said, "I'll check with Richard tomorrow to see if they've turned up anything," referring to the local police chief. Jerry was pretty sure they hadn't started any investigation as it hadn't even been twenty-four hours since Nick was reported missing.

"I appreciate your help on this, Jerry," Austin said, his sincerity coming through clearly in his voice. "I'll see if I can't get the house cleaned up." Silence fell across the cruiser for a short time as both Jerry and Austin seemed to be distracted or otherwise focused. It was Austin who broke the silence. "Why do you think they only opened the cabinet doors and not the drawers?"

"What do you mean?" asked Jerry, his eyes squinting a bit as if trying to hear more clearly.

FALLOUT

"The kitchen cabinets," Austin replied. "All of the drawers were closed. Every one of them." Again a brief silence. "I mean, you've got to assume they didn't open them and then close them back. Every cupboard door, every closet door, every cabinet door was left open." He looked directly at Jerry. "Not one drawer, anywhere in the house, or the garage for that matter, was open when I got there." He turned his head and peered through the passenger side window. "Not one." Silence returned as both men contemplated the questions.

Jerry tried to be reassuring. "We'll find him. We just don't know enough about where to look for him right now." He touched Austin on the shoulder. "He's ok and we'll find him."

About 15 minutes later the sheriff's cruiser turned left onto County Road 45 heading toward Austin's house. While it was a county road, it was still a well maintained motorway with moderately priced homes, new and old, dotted every two or three blocks apart, each separated by short patches of groves, woodland and brush. The homes were close enough to have neighbors but far enough away that you didn't feel like they lived with you.

Austin's home was the fourth house on the left, about two and a half miles from the turn. It was located just around a slight curve in the road and was bordered by wooded land on both sides of the street.

The acreage located across the street from his home was completely undeveloped and showed signs of damage from a recent storm that had passed through a few months ago. It was the downed trees that Austin's eyes were focused on as the car entered the curve and began to slow. Then, his gaze shifted left anticipating his arrival at home.

As the driveway to his home began to appear in the distance, they could see a dark colored Crown Victoria parked on the side of the road closest to Austin's home. Jerry and Austin exchanged a quick glance acknowledging they were both seeing the same thing. The cruiser slowed. The left turn signal flashed on and Jerry eased the car slowly into the driveway while Austin was carefully evaluating the black sedan. He could see two occupants in the car and they, too, were looking at Austin.

The two men in the sedan began to exit their vehicle just as the cruiser came to a stop and Jerry and Austin got out. The driver was a taller, black man who looked to be in his mid-thirties. The other was white, shorter by about half a foot, clearly older than his partner and with a bit more girth, but not really out of shape and Austin felt like he'd seen these two men before. Both men were wearing dark suits with a white shirt and tie and finely shined dress shoes. *A bit hot in Texas to be dressed like that,* thought Austin as the two men approached.

Jerry decided he'd take the lead on this. "Can we help you?" he asked as he stepped around to the rear of the car near the rear passenger door.

With his right hand the taller man reached inside his coat and asked, "Are you Mr. Sims?"

Austin answered, "No. I'm Austin Cole. I live here. Can I help you?"

Pulling his hand from his coat, he flipped open his identification and introduced himself. "Mr. Cole, I'm agent Harris." Pointing to the shorter man on his left he said, "This is my partner, agent Blackwell". The second agent opened his identification as well and held it in place until he saw Austin turn his eyes back to agent Harris. "We're with the NSA and we were hoping we could ask you a few questions." Neither Jerry nor Austin moved.

"Sure," replied Austin. "What's this about?" Jerry moved slightly and leaned against the trunk of the car.

Agent Blackwell spoke up. "Have you recently noticed anything out of the ordinary or unexpected?"

Austin and Jerry had a secret conversation with a simple glance. Jerry could see what was coming. "What?" Austin pointed toward his house. "You mean like my house and garage being broken into?" Deciding more sarcasm was needed, "Or maybe that the whole place was trashed?" Continuing to vent he said, "Or, maybe it's that after all of that," spreading both arms wide, "we can't find my little brother? You mean something out of the ordinary like that?"

The agents looked at each other as if wanting to say something but chose to be steadfast. Agent Blackwell again reached to his inside coat pocket, pulled out his phone, made a few swipes then showed a split shot photo of two men. Agent Harris asked, "Have you seen either of these men around town or at your place of employment?" Agent Blackwell handed the phone with the photo first to Austin and then, out of what seemed like a courtesy, to Jerry.

Austin and Jerry looked carefully at the two photos. The first man was clearly of Asian descent, in his late twenties or early thirties. He had a narrow face with razor stubble, and thin, dark hair. The other man looked a bit older than the first but he was clearly of middle-eastern heritage. Regardless, Jerry and Austin didn't recognize them.

"No. I haven't seen them," Jerry answered and turned his head toward Austin.

"I don't think so," Austin said, trying to be as honest as he could be. "They don't look familiar to me." He looked at the two men inquisitively, one, then the other. "What's this about?"

"We're not at liberty to say," replied Agent Harris. "If you do see them, do not approach them." He handed Austin a card and then another to Jerry. "These are dangerous men. Call us immediately and we'll take it from there."

"So, does this have anything to do with my house being trashed and my missing brother?" Austin asked, hoping the agents might have some information that may help find Nick.

"We don't really know anything about your house being broken into, sir," agent Harris replied.

Jerry couldn't hold back any longer. "What has this," displaying the card, "got to do with Austin? Why do you think he would know who these guys are?"

"We're not at liberty to say, sir." The agents turned to leave then Agent Harris caught himself and turned back to Austin. "Oh, sorry your brother's missing. Hope it turns out alright." The agents walked back to their car, got in and drove away.

CHAPTER EIGHT

Friday, June 12th, 5:41 p.m.:
Cambridge, MA

NSA Field Agent Tim Young had been assigned to maintain surveillance of Kao Yi Szun's apartment so headquarters could be contacted immediately in the event the subject returned. Initially, surveillance was done from his vehicle but with the advance of time it became clear that nearby housing would need to be acquired. This was done and Agent Young had clear view of Kao's apartment. Complete surveillance equipment had been set up to document comings and goings.

At 5:41 p.m. local time the agent noted the arrival of a young Asian woman who had approached the subject's apartments. It was time, he thought, to inform HQ. He picked up his cell phone and dialed directly to Agent Rachael Birch's desk.

"Agent Birch," she answered.

"Agent Birch, this is field-Agent Tim Young," he started. "I have been assigned surveillance in Cambridge concerning OS231 contact subject. I need to report a contact at subject residence."

"Ok, hold on a moment," she said as she changed

screens on her monitor. "Go ahead."

"Contact was Asian female, approximately five foot, six inches tall, perhaps early thirties." He looked again at the apartment. "She knocked on subject's door. No answer. She then made contact with subject's neighbor across the hall." He paused again. "She now appears to be heading to the manager's office."

"Can you get a clear photo of her?"

"I believe so," he replied. "I'll try to get one as she's walking back then email it to you."

"I'll be waiting." Agent Birch hung up the phone.

Seventeen minutes later, an email alert popped up on Birch's monitor and there was the photo as promised. Just as she started to run the photo through facial recognition software her desk phone rang. It was Agent Young calling to confirm that she had received the email and to update her that the woman had left via taxi.

"Contact the cab company and find out where she was picked up and dropped off and get back to me as soon as you have something." Without any social convention the call was ended.

Rachael documented the conversation with agent Young and turned her attention back to the research at hand. The FRS was still running Yi Fun's photo but without results. Meanwhile, Agent Young called the cab company and identified himself then asked for the owner. Once his identification was verified, the owner started checking the logs of the taxi and provided the information to the NSA agent. Fifteen minutes later Agent Young was again on the phone with Rachael Birch.

"The owner of the Cab Company said that the Asian woman was picked up at Lechmere Station at about 4:25 p.m. She was taken directly to the OS231 Contact Subject's apartment. The taxi waited about 10 to 15 minutes while she talked with the manager of the apartment building." Agent Young took a breath then finished his report. "When she returned to the cab the driver took her to Hotel Marlowe where he dropped her off."

"Agent Young, see if you can find out what train she arrived on out of Lechmere Station. Then try to backtrack and find where she first boarded the train." Holding the headset against her ear with her shoulder, she typed the information into her log.

"Yes, ma'am," acknowledged Young.

"Oh," followed Birch, "you know, call immediately when you have something."

When the call ended, Rachael immediately went to her colleagues and asked them to begin looking for video evidence of the young Asian woman. They were requested to find video feed for the Hotel Marlowe and for the arrival at Lechmere Station. "I'll be providing other locations as information comes in."

Each began making inquiries on behave of the NSA immediately, tracking down people with authority to turn over video to the NSA. They had to go through the authentication process with representatives of both the hotel and train station. Some 35 minutes later video was streaming on NSA monitors.

Just as the monitors came alive with separate videos from the two source locations, the call from Agent Young came into Rachael's desk. She had been standing near a monitor at a different station when she heard the phone on her desk ring. She rushed to her desk and picked up the phone. It was, as promised, Agent Young.

"I talked with security at Lechmere Station who took the lead and ended up tracing the Asian back through Harvard Square Station, then back to the Amtrak and ultimately back to JFK where she got on the tram to the Amtrak station around 11:30 p.m."

"Thanks, Agent Young," Birch quickly responded. "We'll take it from here." Birch immediately got in contact with JFK security where once vetted she directed them to start a search for all video evidence of the young Asian. She emailed the photo of Yi Fun, and airport security began their search starting with the estimated time that she got on-board the tram and working their way back, trying to trace her steps back to find what flight she arrived on and thereby the origin of that flight.

While Birch was waiting for a return call from JFK security she called Agent Young to see if he could follow up with the hotel and get them to call immediately if she left the hotel. Hotel security confirmed that she had apparently entered her room around 6:20 p.m. and had not left. Just as the second call from Young was ended, she was buzzed by Director Hughes.

"Any updates on OS231 Contact Subjects, Rachael?"

"I'm running the photo now," she said. "We're maintaining surveillance on subject premises. JFK is running video trying to find out what flight she arrived on. I expect a call from them any minute now."

"Let me know the minute you find out. Oh, and get surveillance on the hotel where she's staying."

"Yes sir." She replaced the headset and continued working. Twenty five minutes later JFK security called to notify her that they were sending customs video of the subject woman entering the country. Just as one monitor was showing the video of Yi Fun at the custom's station, Birch's other monitor sounded an alert to a match. She opened the alert, read it carefully then immediately sprung to her feet and rushed to the director's office.

She didn't knock. "Sir, the contact at OS231 Contact Subject One's residence," she said, placing the report and photo on the desk in front of Director Hughes, "and I don't think you're going to like this."

The Director read the alert. "Suspected MSS Agent!" He stood up quickly. "I want to know where she is, how she knows subject one and what she's got to do with all of this!" He had already started dialing the phone. "Have the agent find out what she wanted from the complex manager. Have him use discretion but definitely identify himself as NSA."

"Have locals secure subject Kao Yi Fun," Director Hughes ordered into the phone. "Target is at Hotel Marlowe. Agent Birch will provide you with room number." He stood and stepped around his desk. "We'll meet in the war room for real-time feed."

Eight minutes later, everyone associated with the operation was in the soundproof conference room, which was lined with electronics and swept for 'bugs' daily. Real-time audio and video from the team at the Hotel Marlowe was coming in and the team had worked their way to the hallway leading to Room 418. The team had gone silent. The team leader gave silent instructions for two men in full protective gear including helmets and face shields to align themselves on either side of the door way. Another member dropped to his knees and slid a thin round wire-shaped line under the door and into the apartment. Moments later the video was displayed on the monitors in the war room.

After a quick, quiet scan of the visible portion of the hotel room, the silent order was given to enter. The team leader took the door key which he had secured from the hotel manager and swiped it in the door reader. There was a slight clicking sound and the LED turned green. The team leader immediately pulled down on the door handle and the two armed men sprung into the room. The first went to the right and into the bath room while looking across the hall-way at the closet. "Clear."

The second stooped and went left to get a clearer view of the suite area. The bed was made and clear. He moved through the room in front of the television and over to the curtains looking behind chairs and curtains. "Clear."

By this time three more men had entered the room, one looking under the bed, another going through the closets and drawers, the third checking everything in the bath. No indication of anyone having been there recently at all. "Clear."

"Damn-it!" screamed the director. "I want her found."

CHAPTER NINE

Saturday June 13th, 5:28 p.m.:
Brookeland, Texas

It had been a strange and tiring day. Jerry had left saying again that he'd check with local police tomorrow and give Austin a call with an update. Meanwhile, Austin was going to spend the rest of the evening trying to put everything back into its place and see if anything was missing, besides his brother that is...

As it was Saturday night and Austin and his friends usually met up and went to the Yellow Rose, a local country bar with a big dance floor, great drinks and a live band, he received a text just before 5:30 p.m. from Butch confirming that they were still going. Austin hadn't had a chance to let the guys know what was going on and in fact, until now had completely forgotten about their plans for tonight. He replied with a text saying that something had come up and he was going to be unable to make it. A few minutes later Austin's cell phone rang. It was Butch.

"What's going on, man?" In the years that Butch had known Austin he'd never cancelled on plans unless he was too sick to go. "Are you ok?"

Austin explained what had happened and what he'd been doing all day and said that he thought he'd just stay in tonight. "Y'all have fun for me."

"No way, man," replied Butch who had another idea. "I'll be right over."

Austin spent a good five minutes trying to talk him out of coming over, giving excuses that in hind sight didn't really make much sense to him much less to Butch. He finally surrendered. "I'll see you when you get here."

About 45 minutes later, as Austin was sitting in the living room going through all the photos that had been dumped and discarded from one of the boxes in his father's bedroom, he caught sight of two vehicles pulling into his driveway, one after the other. He immediately recognized the Mustang as Butch's, and the 2012, metallic-green, Dodge Charger that followed closely behind was Randall's. Austin smiled. *I'll be damned!* Moments later, arms fully loaded with beer, pizza, chips and a bag of something, both men entered the house through the front door and started placing the supplies on any immediately available surface they could find.

"Hope you're decent. Oh hell, what am I saying? Ah, I called Randall," explained Butch. "He said he wanted to come, too, so we decided to pick up a few things."

"I can see that." Austin was abruptly pulled into one hug from Butch and then another from Randall. "Thanks for coming, guys," a hint of a tear beginning to form in his left eye. "It really means a lot."

The guys pulled away, each finding their requisite seating. "No problem, dude," said Randall.

"Yeah," added Butch. "Anything we can do to help, you know we're here."

"Well, as you can see there's a lot to do. They messed things up pretty good."

"I say," said Randall taking the lead, "we eat some pizza before it gets cold then knock this bitch out." All three men agreed but alas, couldn't finish the pizza. *Probably more than we needed,*" Butch thought as he took his last sip of beer. *One more, dead soldier.*

Austin provided some direction and the guys jumped right in, putting things in cabinets, hanging clothes up in closets, creating stacks in each room of things they didn't know what to do with. *What great friends,* Austin thought as each of the guys would pass by with a question about what to do with this or that. Austin saw the house come together so much more quickly than he had expected. And after each trip through the living room each would reward themselves with a leftover, cold slice of pizza and a drink of now warm beer.

By 8:45 p.m. everything was, for the most part, in its place and the guys had settled down in front of the

TV watching something forgettable while finishing off the remaining beer. With each man leaned back and their feet parked firmly on top of the coffee table, the conversation turned to Nick.

"So," started Randall, "what are you going to do now?" Dropping his feet to the floor he reached forward and picked up the bottle sitting in front of him on the coffee table.

"Well, I was supposed to go by the police station Monday and let them know what was missing." Taking a deep breath, Austin continued, "Guess I won't need to do that." They had put everything up and as far as he could tell nothing was missing. "Since nothing was even broken, I don't even think I will need to get a copy of the police report. They said I'd need one for the insurance company."

"Are they trying to find Nick?" asked Butch, still leaning back looking almost asleep.

"They said they would but I got the impression they were just talking," replied Austin. "Jerry said they can't really treat it as a missing person until it's been at least twenty-four hours."

"Well, it's been twenty-four hours, dude," stated Randall.

Austin thought for a moment. "I guess I can go down tomorrow but I doubt there'll be a detective there to talk to." There was a moment of silence. "You know, if I haven't found him by Monday, I'm going to have to take some time off work."

"Did you give them a picture of Nick?" Butch asked.

"No."

"Dude." Randall leaned forward. "They've got to have a recent picture to be able to issue one of those BOLO's!" He hesitated a moment. "Always wanted to say that!" He smiled at Butch and Austin.

Austin took a sip of his beer. "Yep. You're right." He sat the bottle down and continued. "I'll take them one on Monday and I'll see if there's something Jerry can do with one as well."

Having finished his beer, Butch leaned even further back into the sofa and took a big stretch then rocked himself to his feet. "Well guys," he started, "I'm bushed and I'm heading home."

Randall followed suit and stood. "Me, too!" They gathered up their empties and put them in the trashcan just inside the pantry in the kitchen. Austin was standing in front of the recliner waiting as his two friends left the kitchen and walked toward the front door to leave. Each giving Austin a brief hug, the two friends stepped through the doorway and disappeared down the side walk and moments later were gone.

Austin walked through the house locking the doors and shutting off the lights in other rooms then made his way back to the living room, finally letting himself fall into the recliner and exhale. With the recliner foot rest extended Austin took the remote and scanned through the guide to see if anything of interest was on, but nothing could hold his attention. His gaze kept being drawn back to the large stack of folders David had given him, sitting on the end table across the room. Finally he gave up, went over to the table, loaded up the pile of paper and went back to the recliner.

He thumbed through each paper, front and back. He looked at every photo, every printed newspaper article. *Apparently, David and Nick's fascination with the Shuttle disaster was deeply rooted, bordering*, Austin thought, *on OCD*. There were printouts from CNN, Time Magazine, The Washington Post and every local paper in Texas. He found copies of the Shuttle manifest as published by NASA.

According to the manifest this mission involved experiments from the European Space Agency, Israel, Japan, Germany, China and Australia. Austin found detailed descriptions for many of these payloads. There were experiments to study zeolite crystals (*whatever that is,* Austin thought.) There were experiments designed to speed up chemical process and others to enhance genetic characteristics of cells in a weightless environment.

Yellow sticky-notes with David's handwriting

were spread throughout the reports and files. One highlighted a paper describing the nine commercial payloads involving 21 experiments that for some reason David found suspicious as on the note he wrote:

CAN'T FIND A RECORD OF WHO!

Another note simply read "OBPR". *Not sure what that is,* but just as he lifted the note he read, "23 experiments for NASA's Office of Biological and Physical Research." *Oh.* He read on, trying to find out what those experiments were but couldn't find a reference to them anywhere else in the current folder. As he started to close the folder he looked ahead at the heap on the table and saw one folder which stood out near the bottom of the stack. It had a printed label in a clear plastic cover that simply read,

EMPTEC

Someone had taken a yellow hi-liter and placed a line along the upper edge of the folder as if to set it apart from the others. *Well, it worked,* thought Austin as he discarded the other folders and pulled this one from the table. He opened the folder to find documents with so much yellow hi-lite that it was easier to read just those words that were not in yellow. There were sticky-notes on every page and some with many more than one. There were hand-written notes near the borders of every sheet. Austin thought he recognized some of the hand writing as Nick's.

Austin spent the next two hours reading every word, looking at every photo, every graph. He read the notes and later re-read the notes. Everything in this folder had something to do with EMPTEC and its association with STS-107, Space Shuttle Columbia. The EMPTEC was apparently in a highly secretive, fourth phase of testing that required it be conducted in the weightlessness of space. Still, there was no clear definition in anything that Austin had read that indicated exactly what EMPTEC was or what it did or what the experiment criteria was supposed to be.

Wait. I don't remember seeing anything on the manifest about this, Austin thought. He returned to the first folder and flipped through the pages to the manifest. He studied it carefully, then again. *Nope. It's not on here.* He went back to the EMPTEC folder again and found that many of the passages which were hi-lighted referenced the STS-107 mission. *How is that possible?* He started to close the folder again. *How does a highly secretive, unidentified and unassigned payload make it onboard something with as much security in place as the Space Shuttle has around it?*

Just as Austin started to close the front leaf of the

folder he noticed a hand written note on the inside of the leaf. It was hard to read as it was written in pencil against the greyish-brown of the folder jacket, but he could make it out.

P. HC, 205

There was what Austin believed to be a phone number with a Houston, Texas, area code written under it. It occurred to him that maybe he could find what the hand written reference went to inside that folder. This time he revisited the folder looking for anything with P.HC or 205. Again and again he searched every word and every line but couldn't find a match. *Maybe,* he thought, *it's not a thing but maybe rank and initials for a name H.C.?* He began his search again and it didn't take him long. He found a reference to a low-level NASA Payload Manager named Harold Cromwell. *H.C.,* Austin thought.

CHAPTER TEN

Sunday, June 14th, 1:38 a.m.:
Brookeland, Texas

Austin began to wonder if Howard Cromwell was somehow involved or otherwise associated with the mysterious payload of experiments referred to as EMPTEC. He also wondered how he could find out. *Does he still work for NASA? If he doesn't then where is he now?* The wheels were turning and Austin's head felt like it was going to explode. *Maybe it was all the beer.* He looked over at the clock centered on the wall which separated the living room from the bathroom. He read 1:42 a.m. *Oh yeah, time for bed.* Leaving the folders on the table, he headed upstairs and only minutes later he was sound asleep.

The next morning after a quick bowl of cereal, he made his way to the shower, rapidly got dressed and ready to go. He had plans today for finding his brother. He had found a recent photo of Nick that he wanted to take to the local police. He was going to call Jerry and see if he could use it and maybe his department could issue their own BOLO, although he seemed to recall that he'd once been told that one of those had to be issued by the state police. *Doesn't matter*, he thought. *I'm going to try.*

By 2:30 p.m. he had already accomplished the stop at the police station who confirmed that they would send information to the state police for the BOLO. He decided to call Jerry anyway if for nothing else than just to talk. He gave him a brief overview of what he'd found in the folders which no longer seemed as amusing as it did yesterday.

"I think you should go back and have a talk with David," suggested Jerry. "He clearly knows as much about what Nick was doing with this as anyone."

Austin agreed. "Good idea. This stuff is way over my head." He pulled his car into a parking lot for what used to be an ACE Hardware, turned around and headed back toward David's house. Now he wished he'd gotten David's phone number when he was there yesterday. "*Hope he's home.*"

As luck would have it, just as Austin was pulling into the driveway at David's mother's house, both David and his mother were walking toward the home from their car. Both were wearing their Sunday best and were clearly coming home after church *and probably lunch at King's.* His mother went inside but David waited for Austin to catch up to him on the sidewalk.

"Hey, man," David said with his familiar, friendly tone.

Austin saw that David had noticed the arm full of

folders weighing him down as he walked toward the house. "I was hoping you could spare a little bit of time and explain some of this to me," his loaded down, out-stretched arms making it clear to David what Austin was asking.

"Here," offered David. "Let me take some of that." Letting go of half the stack, David and Austin went into the house and again found themselves sitting at the little kitchen table. David's mom had already poured two glasses of lemonade and the guys went right into dissecting the details.

"I've really got so many questions," Austin said, turning pages especially from the EMPTEC folder. "What is EMPTEC and why wasn't it on the manifest published by NASA?" He turned several more pages and pointed to references to experiments in extract-ing and collecting that were directly associated with EMPTEC. "Who was in charge of this? Who owned it? Who developed it? And most importantly, why was Nick so interested?" The questions just came pouring out like David's mother's lemonade into a tall glass.

David finally raised his hand as if to say *STOP*. "Ok. I get it. You have questions." David took a sip of his lemon-ade, reached over and pulled the EMPTEC folder to his side of the table and began to answer what he could. "I'll tell you everything we know and everything we suspect," he said, sporting a suspicious expression on his face.

David opened the EMPTEC folder, shuffled several papers as if he were putting them back into some kind of order that only he was familiar with. "Ok, here it is," taking out two sheets of paper. "We'd been following the search for debris that had been recovered and compared it to the manifest," he said, pulling out several sheets, one of which showed the manifest, the other a list of recovered experiments and another identified debris. "But the thing that caught our attention was that there was so much recovered that was not identified." David continued, "And while there were descriptions for every payload and experiment on the shuttle, there was at least one that no debris was ever found."

David pulled out another sheet located further back in the folder. It was a photograph taken inside of a large warehouse with thousands of pieces of debris, of various sizes and shapes, spread throughout the concrete floor space. Each portion had a raised, plastic number set next to it. He then picked up another sheet with a list of descriptions corresponding to the numbers as listed in the photo. "Nick and I think that we've found connections between many of the listed descriptions of the items in the picture, and the detailed descriptions of the experiments listed on the NASA manifest." He turned it around for Austin to see. He then turned the three pages worth of descriptions of the manifest payloads for Austin to compare.

Austin carefully perused the two documents while David patiently watched. Finally, Austin lifted his eyes toward David. "Ok, so what does this mean?" He turned the pages back around to David who then took one with each hand and held them in the air facing Austin.

"Well, to start with," David raised his eyebrows just a bit, "there are descriptions for all 40,000 unidentified items." Inching his left hand forward toward Austin, "and at the end of each description is a listing of the payload and experiment that NASA believed each piece of debris was associated with."

"So?" Austin said, not following the logic very well.

"There's nothing about EMPTEC." David put down the papers, crossed his arms in front of him and rested them on the table. He leaned in slightly. "We know that there was a payload on that shuttle with an experiment called EMPTEC. It's not listed on the manifest but loading documentation clearly stated it was there."

"Maybe it was something top secret. Maybe it just burned up with most of the rest of the shuttle."

"That's what we thought at first," David replied. "Mission Specialist Kalpana Chawla was a huge fan of Deep Purple and took three of their CD's with her on the trip." David shuffled through the folder again and pulled out a photo then turned it facing Austin. "They found all three of them in a debris field in Nacogdoches."

David picked through the folder again and pulled out one photo, then flipped through the flight manifest again. "There was a biological experiment to study the effects of weightlessness on physiology using worms living in a petri dish." He showed Austin the description from the manifest. "This experiment was only encased in an aluminum canister." David turned the photo toward Austin. "This is a photo of the recovered canister and the living worms recovered on April 28, 2003, almost two full months after the accident."

"Ok, so some CD's and some worms made it out alive." Austin was still confused. "How does any of that apply to EMPTEC?"

"Based on our descriptions of the EMPTEC experiment, it was encased in a large, rugged chamber designed specifically to withstand the kind of environment it would have experienced upon re-entry if the shuttle exploded!"

Austin leaned back in his chair. There were a few seconds of quiet contemplation. "So how do three CD's and bunch of worms in an aluminum canister survive a fiery re-entry and a 39 mile plunge to earth yet they can't find any evidence of an indestructible chamber housing some secret experiment?"

"Exactly!" David collected all the papers and put them back into the folder.

"Unless maybe it's part of the unidentified debris they have found," Austin proposed.

"Except there were descriptions for all 40,000 items and the experiment that they thought the piece of debris was part of." David took a breath then offered, "There were none associated with EMPTEC."

Again a lingering silence. This time David leaned back in his chair. Intentionally leaving the file open, he pushed the chair back and stood for a moment, then picked up his glass and walked to the refrigerator where his mother had left the lemonade. Still, there was silence, only the sound of the lemonade spilling into the glass, the tone getting higher as the glass filled.

"You think it's still out there!" Austin barked. His eyes followed David as he turned to add to Austin's glass.

"That, or it really did disintegrate and they decided not to make any reference to it, ever, anywhere." David put the pitcher of lemonade, now almost empty, back into the refrigerator. "It was clearly classified."

"So what does any of this have to do with Nick's disappearance?"

"The government had search teams out looking for

debris for months after the accident." David sat down. "There were local teams organized everywhere. They called in volunteers, used the National Guard. They even recruited college kids and they looked everywhere from New Mexico to the Mississippi state line." David paused. "But we found a report, where no one was allowed to search, one area that even the National Guard was not allowed to investigate."

The folder on the table, still open, showed a newspaper report of an area where the police and NASA had warned everyone to stay away because of the potential for hazardous materials in the debris in that area. David glanced down at the report. Austin's eyes followed David's.

"As far as Nick and I can tell only eight specialized teams were allowed in during the quarantine. Eight teams to search over 180 square miles. Apparently, they did it in four days."

"Where?"

"In a rural area just outside of Nacogdoches."

"How do you know all of this?" asked Austin.

"Nick and I actually interviewed some of the people who lived in the area," David explained. "Most were tight-lipped but we did find out how long they were out of their homes."

"Bottom line," Austin was now ready for something specific. "Did they find EMPTEC or not?"

"We don't know," David answered. "What we do know is who we think was heading up the search and recovery for that area and who was in charge of overseeing the recovery, identification and storing process."

Another pause. Austin's eyes widened. "Payload Manager, Howard Cromwell!"

CHAPTER ELEVEN

Sunday, June 14th, 6:45 p.m.:
Brookeland, Texas

By 6:45 p.m. Austin was back home and settling in for the rest of the evening. He didn't feel as though he'd made any progress in locating Nick and wasn't feeling very optimistic anything positive would happen anytime soon. Even though it was Sunday evening he decided to go ahead and call his boss and let him know what was happening and that he'd need to take some time off. That accomplished, he sat back in his recliner and went through David's files again, having decided to bring them back home with him just in case.

Harold Cromwell, Austin thought. *He's got to be tied into this somehow.* Austin remembered the phone number that Nick had written on the sticky-note. He thought for a moment. *Why not!* He reached for the phone and started dialing and waited as the phone rang several times without an answer. *I'll try again tomorrow,* he thought as he hung up the phone.

Again, he leaned back in his chair still looking at the sticky-note. *P H.C. 205,* he read. *If H.C. is Harold Cromwell, then what is the P for and what about 205?* He started brainstorming. His eyes were sweeping the room for inspiration. He glanced up at the television and watched the commercial currently airing. Nothing was helping. He got up out of the recliner and started into the kitchen for another beer when he noticed one of Nick's textbooks from Lawson Technical Institute where he learned welding.

Wait a minute! He froze in place. Speaking out loud he said, "He's a professor!" He quickly turned back to the table and picked up the folder. He flipped it open, looking for information on Harold Cromwell. He couldn't find anything current. Then he remembered the phone number: it was a Houston phone number. He needed a computer and the only one they had in the house was Nick's, and it was gone. Knowing he'd have to find a computer and he would not be able to do that until tomorrow, he closed the folder, kicked back in the recliner, raised his feet and watched television. He felt pretty good that finally, now, he had a plan.

Monday morning Austin got up early just as though he were going to work. He took his shower, had his coffee, both cups at home this time, and knowing the library wouldn't be open until 9:00AM he sat down, took up a pad and pen and decided to write down what he knew about Harold Cromwell. After a lot of looking back through the folders and a little writing, by 8:15 a.m. he felt like he had everything he knew, in a nutshell. All he had to do was find out where Mr. Cromwell was now.

He grabbed his pad and pen, an extra cup of coffee, the folder and the keys to his truck and he was off to the library. He still arrived about 10 minutes before the library opened but that afforded him the opportunity to finish off the last of his coffee and clear his head. *If I had a smart phone I wouldn't have to do this,* Austin thought as he exited his truck and started toward the door of the building. He arrived just seconds after the door was unlocked and followed the librarian as she walked back and behind her station.

Austin headed straight for the computers and sat down at the first one. He used the provided log-on and began his search. He started searching for an address for Mr. Harold Cromwell living in or near the Houston area code given in the phone number. The search results returned three H. Cromwell's, but the phone numbers did not match. Then he tried a search for P.H. Cromwell. Still the returns were negative. Just as he was about to give up he remembered that Cromwell was retired and that the P may represent Professor. He typed in the web address for the University of Houston, then started looking through faculty until finally, there it was: Professor Harold Cromwell, Room 205 of the Physical Sciences Building. Austin left so quickly he almost forgot to log off the computer.

It took Austin a little over three and a half hours

to drive to Houston and locate the Physical Sciences building. Once parked, he headed up the stairs to the doors of Learner Hall only to find that proper ID was required to gain access to this building. It was clear that this would be a dead end. *Only one place to go,* Austin concluded.

He set his GPS to the street address that Nick had listed under Cromwell's name and started out. GPS said that it would take him an estimated 25 minutes to get there. Seeing that it was well after lunch he decided to stop and get a burger before driving over. Forty-five minutes later he turned into Shady Acres Estates and two blocks later he was turning up the street toward a modest brick home with a nicely landscaped yard and a detached, two-story, two-car garage. *No Cars.* Clearly Cromwell wasn't home so Austin pulled down the street and over to the curb so that he could see through his rear view mirror when he arrived.

After a few minutes of waiting, he decided he'd take a walk, stretch his legs and maybe just take a peek in the windows from the front porch. Stepping out of his truck, he shook his legs to wake them up, closed the door and walked around to the sidewalk. He walked slowly as if just enjoying the sunshine. It was a hot, sunny day as was typical for June and he was thankful he'd chosen to wear khaki shorts and a tee-shirt. *Could have made for an uncomfortable day,* he thought as he strolled up the sidewalk bordering the street toward Mr. Cromwell's home.

As he came nearer the home of Mr. Cromwell, he started evaluating the homes adjacent and nearby to see if there was any activity. He didn't want to look too suspicious. The streets and yards being all but deserted, he turned up the sidewalk leading to the porch then up the stairs. Even though he knew Mr. Cromwell was not home he knocked on the door hoping that perhaps his wife was home or better still, no one would be there. When no one answered he went to each of the windows on the porch and peered in to see what he could see. *Nothing out of the ordinary,* he thought, as he stepped back from the windows and turned toward the stairs. *Guess I'll just wait him out in the truck,* he thought, walking down the stairs toward the street. *It couldn't be that much longer.*

He glanced at his watch. Suddenly, he heard a screeching of ties and the powerful roar of an accelerating engine coming from down the street to his left. The black SUV strained to stay upright as it made the turn onto Mr. Cromwell's street then leveled off as the driver gunned the engine heading straight for Austin.

In seconds the SUV was nearing the house and again the scream of the tires as the vehicle skidded to a halt directly ahead of Austin as he was walking toward his truck. Austin stopped in his tracks realizing somehow this was about him. Immediately, the two rear passenger doors and the front passenger door to the SUV swung open. Three large, stocky, well-armed men surrounded him, each wearing all black clothing, what looked like bullet proof vests and black ski masks on their heads but not pulled down over their faces. Two of the men grabbed Austin by each arm. The third stood watch, his right hand poised on the holstered weapon at his side.

"What's this all about?" Austin screamed. "Who are you?" There was no reply.

The two men forced Austin into the back seat, one sliding in beside him while the other hurried around to the other side. The third man kept watch until they were inside then got into the front, passenger side seat and quickly closed the door. There was a fourth man behind the wheel who never left the vehicle and had already started to speed off before each of the three men had completely closed their doors.

Once inside the SUV the two men started to put a hood over Austin's head. Austin resisted as the two men wrestled to get the hood on. Finally, the larger man to Austin's right dropped his hands and the hood to the seat.

"Look," he started, "you can wear the hood so that you won't know where you're going," he paused, "or..." He pulled his holstered side arm forward a bit. "Your call."

Austin slouched a bit then lowered his head. "Wait!" His head stood tall again. "I've seen you." He looked to his right. "You'll have to kill me anyway," he both stated and asked.

"All you've seen are a few guys that even if you described us perfectly, they'd never be able to find." He turned his head a bit and opened his arms, "And with no harm done, they're going to be less than motivated to spend any time looking for some guys without names, fingerprints, addresses or any evidence other than just your description."

Austin thought for a moment. *Makes sense. Damn it!* "Ok," he said, "put it on." Seconds later everything went dark. For what seemed like half an hour they drove. He could feel the bumps of the road. He counted two turns to the left then one to the right. Then, there was a long stretch where he could feel them go through curves, speed up and slow down but never coming to a complete stop. Finally, they slowed, made a few turns. After the long drive Austin had kind of lost focus of the number of turns, but it seemed to him there was a right turn, short, bumpy drive, right turn, slightly longer, bumpier drive, then a left turn and the SUV came to a stop. Not one word was spoken by any one during the entire drive. *Come to think of it, I don't even remember hearing any sound!*

Austin heard the doors open then he heard the man

to his right slide off the seat. He felt someone grab his right arm above the elbow and lightly pull, like he was being politely told to exit the vehicle but without any words. Still wearing the hood, Austin was ushered about 15 steps, and then led through a doorway. He felt his left arm brush against the door handle. He took another 25 to 30 steps before he was slowed, then the hand on his arm went to his shoulder and out came the first words he'd heard spoken in over half an hour. "Sit."

After sitting for a few hours, hood over his face, his hands behind his back and tied to the chair back near the seat and his leg securely tied just above the ankle to the bottom of the chair legs, he was beginning to feel the stiffness of inactivity invade his body. Just as he started to call out for someone, anyone, he heard the creaking of a door with rusted hinges begin to open. The sound reverberated all around him. He heard footsteps echo through the building. He straightened himself; found some composure. *Must be a large empty building,* he thought, trying to listen more carefully. *Clearly coming from my right, rear, must be three or four.* He caught himself almost smile. R*eally, that's just a guess based on the number of guys in the truck!*

The footsteps began to slow as they came closer. Austin could tell that at least one person walked past him and stopped somewhere in front of him. The others seemed to stop at different spots around him. The smells of old motor oil and mildew were briefly wiped away by the smell of cologne as once again someone approached him from his front left. Apparently close, Austin felt the ropes around his wrists jiggle as if they were being checked for effectiveness.

"Are the ropes too tight?" asked a voice with a very strong foreign accent. "Do they make you uncomfortable?"

Maybe he was emboldened knowing his captors did not intend to kill him. Maybe it was his impatience and irritation having built up for so long that he no longer cared, but his response was embittered. "Don't know where you come from buddy, don't really care," he said quickly but calmly, "but, I'm just a simple man who doesn't get kidnapped and tied to a chair very often, so," he paused briefly, "yes, I'm uncomfortable."

The foreigner stepped away slightly, let a brief smile creep across his face. "Unfortunate, but necessary, I assure you," he responded. "My hope is that you will provide us with your full cooperation and that this will all be over soon so as to not prolong your discomfort."

Not really feeling any less concerned, Austin asked, "What do you want from me?"

"Well, Meester Cole," he paused. "Yes, we know precisely who you are. And we believe that you can tell us where we may find EMPTEC." He spoke the word with emphasis and, Austin thought, a certain dramatic flair.

"I don't know where it is," Austin decried. "Hell, I just heard the word EMPTEC for the first time yesterday!"

"And, what did you find out yesterday, Meester Cole?" the voice asked as though he only half believed his statement.

"Look," Austin started to explain, "my brother's missing and..." A striking blow across Austin's left cheek left a burning sensation and interrupted his speech.

"I do not care about your brother!" his captor obviously irritated and impatient followed up the slap. "I want to know, where is EMPTEC? Nothing more."

Austin was trying to shake off the pain of the slap and took a breath. "That's what I'm trying to explain." He took a deep breath. "I don't know where...."

Again a blow to his right cheek only this time harder with what felt like a closed fist. He almost passed out. Maybe it was the pain that kept him conscious. It didn't matter. Just as he started to raise his head, another punishing punch was thrown to his chin. He could feel the blood pooling in his mouth and sneaking through to his lips.

"Meester Cole," came the exaggerated accent. "I know you. I know Meester Cromwell, former Payload Manager for NASA. I know EMPTEC experiments." He paused as he walked over to Austin, putting his face directly in front of Austin's, so close that he could feel his breath through the hood he was still wearing. "What I want to know from you is the location of the canister."

Austin slowly shook his head. "I don't....." Another bone crushing punch to his right jaw near his ear. He could feel himself slowly losing consciousness.

"Perhaps, Meester Cole," the voice said more calmly, "I will let your wounds get to know you. Perhaps after a while of talking with your pain you will be more willing to talk openly with us."

Austin was barely conscious long enough to hear the shoes start to shuffle as the men casually walked away, leaving him humped-over, a limp heap with only the ropes holding him upright.

CHAPTER TWELVE

Sunday, June 14th, 8:33 p.m.:
NSA Headquarters, Maryland

Agent Rachael Birch had spent the first six hours of her Sunday going over all of the security video from the hotel from the time between the taxi dropping Kao Yi Fun off at the hotel and when the assault team entered her room. She had clear video of the young Asian entering the hotel, walking to the elevator, getting off at her floor, walking the hallway to Room 418 and walking in. She could not find any evidence that she ever left that room.

"Find anything?" asked Agent Greg Benton as he walked past Birch's station on his way to his own.

"No. Nothing," she replied, the frustration clearly coming through in her voice. "She never left!"

Still walking the few steps to his station, he commented in passing, "Maybe she went out the window." He plopped down in his chair. "She is, after all, a trained MSS agent. Maybe she's an acrobat, too." He smiled and turned to his monitors.

Birch dismissed the poor attempt at humor and went back to studying the videos. She suddenly paused.

Wait a minute, she thought. *What if she did go out the window?* She picked up the phone and called the two agents who had secured the hotel video. She wanted them to find external video from any building in the area with an angle that might include a view of Room 418.

She didn't get the videos until almost 3:30 p.m. and there were massive amounts of footage to go through. Even with the help she recruited from tech support it still took over two hours to compile the singular video that she would need. Finally it was done and Agent Birch grabbed the laptop and rushed to Director Hughes's office.

"This is what we've found so far, sir," she said as she placed the laptop on the top left corner of his massive oak desk. The screen was split into four frames. "These camera angles are from the Bryant Bank building, here," she pointed. "Foxx Photography from the east." She pointed again. "These two are the Gulf Station at the corner of Fifth and Lindsey and the Dress Shop Design just three blocks from Land Boulevard." She stepped back from the laptop slightly. "We have them sequenced," she said as she leaned forward then pressed the enter key.

The upper left screen began playing. "This is the Bryant Bank building at 9:08 p.m. If you look at the upper right hand corner you can see a figure climbing down the wall of the hotel." The figure made their way from floor to floor, climbing left then down then right then down until the video lost sight near the bottom of the second floor. The video stopped.

The next video started in the upper right hand corner. "This is Foxx Photography," she pointed again at the lower left hand corner of the active screen window, "and you can see it picked up the same figure walking along Land toward Fifth Street." The video was segmented and short. "You can see that a cab was waiting for her here."

Director Hughes interrupted her. "Bob, get all of the phone records from Room 418 from between the hours of 6:00 p.m. and 9:00 p.m." He looked back at the computer screen. "Go on."

Birch continued. "The cab apparently dropped her off at DuPont and Sixth Street then drove off." She pointed to the final video which was already running. "And now she's walking down Nunley back toward Fifth Street. As you can see this is time stamped 9:48 p.m. We lose her here."

The director looked up, thought for a moment, then asked, "Ok, so where is she going, any ideas?"

"Interesting, sir. Subject Contact One, in the case of OS231, resides just a few blocks from that location," Birch replied. "It can't be a coincidence that she visited the apartment earlier that day then shows up near there, walking in that direction just a few hours later after it's conveniently gotten dark."

"Contact the surveillance agent assigned to subject's residence. See if he's seen her tonight," commanded the director.

"Already on it, sir," said Birch. "He's checking video now. He said he didn't see anything but maybe video did."

"So why would she go back to his apartment?" It was obvious the director was brainstorming and encouraging others in the room to do so as well.

"Well, sir," Agent Bob Matthews offered, "While she did go to the residence, there is no evidence that she actually got to go inside." Every eyebrow raised. "Maybe she needed to get inside. Maybe she's looking for something."

"There's nothing in there. We've already searched that apartment top to bottom and found nothing," retorted Agent Birch.

"Yes, but she may not know that!"

Director Hughes stood. "Birch, have your surveillance agent interview the apartment manager again. See if there's something more she remembers." Hughes walked from behind the desk and put his hand on Matthews's shoulder as if leading him from the room. "Get a team over there and go through that apartment again."

Matthews withdrew as Hughes turned back to

his desk. Agent Birch had collected her laptop and was turning to leave when Hughes again stopped her. "Better still, why don't you go visit the manager along with your agent?" he suggested in a tone that seemed more direct. "While I know that you aren't an experienced field agent, I think you may catch something that the field guy might miss. You need to be there early; no later than 9:00 a.m." As Director Hughes sat down in his chair Agent Birch was walking through the doorway to his office feeling both excitement and a bit of apprehension.

Monday morning after about a three hour drive to Cambridge, Agent Birch pulled up in front of the apartment manager's office, shut off the engine and looked for Agent Young's vehicle. Just as they had planned, Agent Young had parked on the same side of the street as the office and flashed his lights upon Rachael's arrival.

Both Agents exited their respective vehicles at the same time. Agent Young stood by the right rear fender of his car and buttoned his suit coat while waiting for Rachael to cross the street, then both agents approached the door to the manager's office. Rachael knocked twice.

"Come in," came the voice from the other side of the door. "It's open."

Agent Young opened the door and allowed Agent

Birch to enter first. Each agent reached inside their blazers for their identification as the manager stood and said, "Hi. I'm Cindy Moore. So how can I help you two?"

"Ma'am," Rachael took lead. "I'm Agent Birch of the NSA." Pointing to Tim she added, "This is Agent Young."The manager's body immediately became stiff, the brightness she had exhibited when they entered all but gone now. "We'd like to ask you a few questions about a visitor you had last Friday. She was a young, Asian woman. Do you recall meeting this woman?" Rachael presented the manager with a photo of Kao Yi Fun.

"Yes. Yes I do. She came looking for her brother who rents one of our apartments."

"Did she say why she was looking for him?" asked Agent Birch.

"She said he hadn't been answering his cell. She said that she'd been calling him for weeks but he never answered and never returned her messages."

"Did she ask you for anything in particular?"

"Well, she asked to be let into his apartment but I can't really do that." She looked at both agents then added, "Because that's illegal."

"What did she do after you said no?"

"She seemed ok with it. In fact, she paid his rent," the cheery personality beginning to show itself again, "which was almost four weeks late. I thought I was going to have to take action, you know?" She smiled briefly. "Oh, and I let her look at his mail." Realizing what she'd said she quickly added, "I didn't let her open any of it. She just thought it might give her a clue where he might have gone."

"Do you still have his mail?" Birch asked. "And if you do can we have a look as well?"

"I sure do." She pulled open the drawer and took out the mail now wrapped with a thick, large rubber band, then handed it to Agent Birch. "You know, there really wasn't anything in there when she looked." Rachael was thumbing through each envelope, checking postmarks, return addresses, and special markings. Cindy was trying to be more helpful as they looked. "Although," she added, "she did find one envelope interesting. It was marked...."

Agent Birch interrupted the manager, "Return to sender?"

"Why, yes!" the stunned manager replied as Rachael handed the envelope to Young.

Young lay the envelope down on a clear area of the manager's desk. Agent Birch walked up with her phone and took a photo, picked the envelope up off the desk and handed it back to the manager.

"Thank you for your help, ma'am," Rachael said as she pulled a card out of her pocket and handed it to the manager. "Please call us immediately if anyone else contacts you about this or if either of the two subjects returns."

"You bet," said the manager with a sigh of relief.

As the two NSA agents walked out of the office Agent Birch took her cell phone in her right hand and speed-dialed the director's office line. When the director answered, Rachael was direct. "I think she's headed to Houston, sir."

"Have your agent stay there in case her brother returns. Get to the airport now. We'll have a plane ready for you when you get there. You get to Texas, meet up with Harris and Blackwell. They'll pick you up at the airport in Houston." He finished with, "And Rachael, find her."

CHAPTER THIRTEEN

Monday, June 15th 11:00 p.m.:
Somewhere outside Houston, Texas

Austin had been awake for what he guessed was about an hour. He had no clue how long he'd been out but he did know he was hurting; really hurting. There was the sticky feeling of dried blood that had trickled down the side of his face and down his neck. He could feel the beginnings of a scab near the corners of his mouth and both eyelids were heavy from the swelling. He couldn't breathe very well through his nose and it hurt when he opened his mouth to breathe and the air whisked over his swollen lips. He could no longer feel the tension in his wrists or ankles. *I wonder if that's because I've lost circulation,* he thought, *or if it's just that everything else hurts too much for my body to notice the rest.*

Straining, he tried to see through his swollen eyes and the hood over his face to get a feel for how long he'd been out. *Looks like the sun has gone down so it must have been three or four hours,* he deduced. He started wondering if anyone was around but didn't want to call out, thinking that it may bring them back for another round. He listened carefully, fighting through the pain, holding his breath as long as he could, trying to hear the slightest sound. Nothing except what he thought might be the wind blowing through holes in the walls of the old, abandoned building.

At first he wasn't sure but he thought he'd heard a brief, faint swoosh as though someone had taken a deep breath. He waited only a second. There. There it was. There was a distinct sound as if a broom were lightly brushing the floor. *Maybe,* he thought, *more like being carefully placed.* And from the slight brushing sound, he figured it must be fairly heavy. Again he strained, holding his breath, ever-so-slightly turning his head from one side to the other, trying to figure out, subtle and quiet as it had been, what direction the noise may have been coming from.

He heard no sound. He waited. Then he felt a faint whisper of a breeze as though the wind direction had momentarily changed then returned. He could feel warmth near his shoulder and chest, and then felt something slip slowly up under the hood and gently raise it over his eyes. It took several seconds for his battered eyes to adjust and focus but eventually the haze faded away. Kneeling directly in front of him was a small hooded form, all in black with their left hand holding up Austin's hood and their right hand holding a single index finger over what would be their mouth.

Austin didn't say a word. He was not even sure he was breathing. The dark figure reached down to the ropes holding Austin's ankles to the chair legs and worked them loose. Austin stretched his legs forward as the masked figure moved around to the back of the chair and released his wrists. Austin leaned forward as if trying to get up. In an instant his rescuer was to his front, right side and holding their index finger over Austin's swollen lips.

With one arm around his back and waist, his liberator took his right arm and placed it over their shoulder to help Austin stand up. Slowly they worked their way through the dark, mildew-laden warehouse. Austin was hoping this helper could see more clearly than he because he couldn't tell where they were going. The more they moved the more Austin's leg recovered some strength and the less heavy he felt. They stopped at one point, with Austin leaning against a vertical I-beam support.

Again with the presentation of the 'quiet' sign, he was suddenly alone. He looked around the beam and could make out a dim form of a door way where the walls had been silhouetted by the moonlight. He saw the movement of a dark figure at the doorway, then sudden movement outside. He could clearly make out a large, white man as he walked by the open doorway.

Austin's eyes were fixed on the doorway as the

masked figure darted through the doorway immediately after the man had passed by. They both disappeared for a moment then with a thud Austin saw
the big man fall backward and the small, dark figure
walk past and back in through the door. *Tough little guy,*
Austin thought, as the hooded figure grabbed him once
again. In a flash with his savior's assistance they were
making their way through the door and out into the
deserted, overgrown parking area.

After being guided around the limp, prostrate,
unconscious body just outside the door, Austin was
leaned against the sole SUV that was parked just a
few feet away. He could barely hold himself upright
as he watched his rescuer slash both the front and rear
tires on the passenger side of the SUV. Austin was then
ushered off toward the back of the building and into
what was apparently at one time a large lay-down area
for materials. Now it was overgrown with chest high
grasses, bushes and small trees.

They made their way across the darkened field, over
a fallen fence and then around another abandoned facil-
ity until they were out of site of the warehouse and his
captors. Just as they went past the front corner of the
manufacturing building Austin could see a smaller office.
He began to move a bit more quickly now and as he went
by the office he could see he was being led to a small dark
car parked near the curb in front of the building.

His emancipator directed him to the car and had the passenger side door open when he arrived. Once he was helped into his seat, his partner deliberately and quietly pulled the handle of the door open while pressing it closed. Austin was not even sure the door had shut all the way and had almost started to reopen it to slam it shut but decided to wait. *He must have a reason,* Austin thought. *Probably didn't want to risk making too much noise.....Duh!*

In a flash the driver was in the car having quietly shut his door as well. The car was started, motor revved and the car sped off as quickly as possible while still being careful not to screech the tires. Two turns, a couple of short straightaways, lots of bumps and another turn then finally they were on the open highway and the gas pedal hit the floor throwing Austin back into his seat. Just as the speed started to level out, yet still disquietingly fast, the driver reached up and pulled off the hooded mask.

"Are you ok?" asked Yi Fun, glancing at Austin while running her right hand through her long black hair several times to release the tangles. "Are you ok?!" she asked again as Austin seemed disoriented and speechless.

"Yes," he finally replied. He stared at Yi Fun for a few seconds then blurted, "You're a girl!" He seemed to be both asking and stating, his surprise evident. "Who are you?" He turned slightly in his seat so that he could see her more clearly out the least swollen eye. "Why did you help me?"

"My name is Kao Yi Fun." She seemed to pay little attention to Austin as she was still driving feverishly. Her eyes checked the side mirrors and then the rear-view, but not trusting what she saw, she stole a glance back over her shoulder and looked through the rear window. There were no headlamps and there didn't seem to be anyone following. She seemed to inhale then brought the speed of the vehicle under control.

"Where are we going?" Austin asked as he pulled his seat belt across his chest and locked it into place.

"We have to get you some bandages to treat your wounds," she said, pointing to the cuts over his eyes and cheek bones. "Then we'll go somewhere safe. I will answer your questions then."

Austin had leaned back into his seat, the pain beginning to take precedence over the adrenaline rush from the rescue. They had been driving for about thirty minutes and had managed to find what Austin thought was one of the most deserted city streets he'd ever seen. Having driven southwest of Houston away from the city, the only light in the car came from the illuminated dash. Every now and then they would pass a rural home with outside security lights but for the most part, it was just dark. That made it easy for Austin to fall asleep.

He was awakened as the car slowed and turned into a parking lot of a mom-and-pop gas station that looked to be getting ready to close. The parking lot was all but empty and while the lights were on and the open sign proudly displayed, Austin wasn't really sure there was anyone here. The car came to a stop near the front of the building but parked sideways pointing away. *In case we need to leave in a hurry,* Austin thought.

Yi Fun unbuckled her seatbelt and opened the door. "Stay here," she said as she turned to get out of the car. "I'll be back in a moment." Austin was good with that. He wasn't sure he could get out anyway.

Moments later Yi Fun opened her door and pitched two bags into the back seat, got behind the wheel, buckled up and again they were off. Continuing on the same highway for another 20 minutes it only got darker, later and more painful for Austin. Yi Fun glanced over at him as he seemed to be writhing a bit and tapped his left arm.

"There is pain medication and a soft drink in one of the bags in the back seat." Realizing he was probably unable to reach the bags she slipped her right arm back around her seat and snapped up the two bags, pulled them into the front seat and placed them into Austin's lap. She again looked over at him. "Can you open the drink?" Her eyes alternated between watching the road and watching Austin's sluggish movement.

FALLOUT

Austin reached into a bag and pulled out the drink in a plastic bottle with a twist off cap. "No problem," he said, as he twisted the lid of the bottle and immediately took a long gulp. He then dug around and found the pain medication, popped off the top, then fought with the protective seal. Once the seal was off he dumped three capsules into his hand and directly into his mouth, chased immediately with the drink. Then he just leaned his head back.

A sudden lunge of the car and a series of shakes rattled Austin from his slumber. He took a quick inventory of his surroundings: Yi Fun still driving. It was still dark and they were still in the middle of nowhere. Only this 'nowhere' was a dirt, pothole-laden parking lot to another deserted warehouse that looked like an old automotive repair shop. Yi Fun was heading straight for the front door.

As the car came to a stop and the lights and motor shut off, both Yi Fun and Austin surveyed the old shop. It was hard to see but there looked to be a corn field or something surrounding the building on three sides with old, rusted trucks and cars planted at several places around the building, each in varying stages of disintegration. There were no lights, no people, and no animals that either could make out.

"Get out," Yi Fun instructed as she opened her door and stepped out.

Austin had barely gotten to his feet when Yi Fun opened the door and disappeared inside. He locked and shut his door and walked to the old shop, stood at the entrance and stared into the darkness straining to finding Yi Fun in a sea of blackness. He started to call out but thought better.

"Come in," said Yi Fun's voice from somewhere deep into the shop.

"How? I can't really see anything." A moment later, Yi Fun turned on a small flash light. She was stooping in a corner and tightly held the miniature light between her inner thighs, careful that the light did not escape the spot it created on the floor. "Oh!" Austin found his way to the light. "What now?" he asked as he stooped beside her on the floor.

"You stay here. Do not make any noise." She turned off the light and stood. "I must seal any openings that may give away our presence here."

Austin sat quietly waiting for her to return. Several times during his wait he heard slight noises but nothing really loud. Then just as suddenly as she had gone Yi Fun was again on the floor beside Austin with the flashlight on and no need to hide the beam. She carried a small open-top can, some paper and small debris.

"What's that for?" he asked as he pointed at the pile she'd placed on the floor.

"We need a fire for light. Then I need to clean and

bandage your wounds," she said, pointing at the cuts above his eyes, cheek and mouth. Having started the fire, she poured out the contents of the two bags from the convenience store, spread everything out, and said, "This is going to hurt."

CHAPTER FOURTEEN

Tuesday, June 16th, 12:57 a.m.:
Somewhere outside Houston, Texas

"How do I explain this to my employers, Samir? You let him escape!" The small, well-dressed Moroccan paced to his left and right. Sometimes he walked around behind the focus of his outrage.

"I did not let him escape, Mehdi! I swear it!" Samir Halimi countered.

"You fell asleep and he managed to escape!" Mehdi El Azzouz screamed at his henchman, standing so close that spit actually sprinkled Samir's face.

Sitting in the same chair that had only recently held Austin Cole as his prisoner, Samir tried to explain. "Someone helped him. I had just finished patrolling the highway side of the building and turned to go past the door to the opposite side." He lowered his eyes. "Just as I got near the truck I felt a blow to my stomach. Next there was a blow to my head. That's the last thing I remember." He opened his arms slightly. "The next thing I know is that you were standing over me."

Just as Samir had finished, another member of their team walked up to Mehdi and quietly said, "Both tires have been slashed. There is one spare."

"Take a spare from one of the others. See if one of them will work," instructed Mehdi. He stepped back from Samir a bit and put his right hand to his chin. "So, the obvious questions are: How do we reacquire our Meester Cole? Who is helping him and why?" He casually looked at both men before him not really expecting an answer.

Mehdi El Azzouz was a powerful, decisive man with a large bank account and a willingness to do whatever was necessary to maintain that lifestyle. He surrounded himself with a team of mercenaries responsible for his safety and basically anything else they were instructed to do.

Samir Halimi was perhaps his most experienced henchman. He had served in the military for several years before becoming a professional mercenary. He was tall, muscular, knew his weapons and was perhaps best at hand-to-hand combat.

Farid Tsouli was a smaller man with a slender, less muscular build whose specialty was firearms. He was an expert marksman with both a hand gun and rifle. To Medhi, one of Farid's most endearing qualities was his unflinching willingness to kill.

For this undertaking Medhi knew he needed someone with more subtle talents and mechanical as well as technical mindset. That's where Younes El Aroud came in. He was well educated and had a gift with computers, games, basically anything with electronics. It was those talents that lead to Younes as the choice to resolve their current tire issue.

Deciding that he was not going to let a flat tire stop him from achieving his goal, Medhi dropped his hand from his chin, turned and walked outside to the twin Cadillac Escalades parked in front of the warehouse. His two associates were unsure if they should follow. Samir stood but hesitated to see if Farid would go as well. When Farid started following Mehdi, Samir moved quickly to keep pace but still let Farid lead the way.

"How much longer before you are finished?" Medhi asked. Younes, who was sitting at the rear of the damaged Escalade, had put one tire on and was tightening the lug nuts.

"Perhaps 20 minutes," he replied.

"Make it 10," Medhi demanded. He then turned his attention back to Samir and Farid. "Go collect all of our gear. Leave nothing behind. Put everything into the trucks." He walked over to Samir and stood almost nose to nose. "Do not fail me. Any trace will lead the authorities to us. Surely they have already been alerted when we took Meester Cole." Medhi turned back to the Escalades.

Just before the two men began to leave, Samir

stopped and asked, "Where will we be going, Medhi?"

After a brief but intense pause Medhi turned and gave Samir a piercing stare. "We will return to Meester Cromwell's in hopes that our Meester Cole will return." He again moved in closer to Samir. "It would be most fortuitous for you if he does."

CHAPTER FIFTEEN

Monday, June 15th, 4:30 p.m.:
Houston, Texas

It took the private NSA jet a little over four hours to fly directly from Massachusetts to Houston, where as promised Agents Harris and Blackwell were waiting when Agent Birch exited the plane at the hanger bay. Blackwell had already opened the rear, driver's side door as Rachael had taken her last step down the stairs and onto the tarmac. She walked straight to the black Crown-Vic and settled in. Moments later, the three NSA agents were on their way.

"Cromwell's residence is about 35 minutes from here," offered Agent Harris as he drove out of the airport and onto the highway. "We should get there around 5:00."

Rachael took the time to fill the guys in on what had transpired; the abbreviated version, of course, but with enough detail that the guys could read in the rest. "So, we don't know why she's here except that she's clearly looking for her missing brother."

"Interesting," exclaimed Agent Blackwell. "We met a man the other day at OS231 Subject Caller Two's home address whose brother was also missing."

"Any connection with our target?" asked Rachael.

"Don't know," he replied. "But, it is curious. The thing is, we think the missing brother was Subject Caller Two"

"That is not a coincidence," Rachael stated matter-of-factly.

Just as Rachael had finished the sentence Agent Harris turned onto the street where Harold Cromwell lived in Shady Acres Estates. As the turn began to straighten the agents could see flashing red, yellow and blue lights coming from just beyond the Cromwell residence. Slowing the car as they approached, they saw a wrecker and a local police car. Between the two vehicles sat an older model Ford F150 pickup truck.

"No one in the truck or the police cruiser," Blackwell observed.

"Let's find out what's going on," said Rachael. Agent Harris drove past the wrecker and parked just ahead of it and to the side of the street. All three agents got out of the car and walked toward the police officer who was in deep conversation with the operator of the wrecker.

Rachael reached into her jacket pocket as she approached the police officer who had finally noticed her, and pulled out her identification. "Hi. I'm Agent Rachael Birch of the NSA." Pointing to them, she introduced the other two agents. "This is Agent Harris and Agent Blackwell." Looking around while replacing their ID's Rachael added, "So, what's going on here?"

"Apparently we had a kidnapping here," the officer explained. "The neighbors said they saw a man in his thirties, about six foot one walking toward this truck and suddenly a black SUV with at least three men just drove up, grabbed him and sped off. Threw his cell phone out the window. IT Forensics has it now. CSI has the rest."

Agent Birch reached into her coat pocket and pulled out one of her cards and handed it to the officer. "Would you please have them send me any fingerprint results they find immediately? They can send it to my office. I'll have someone there do some digging." Before he answered she looked over to the Cromwell residence and asked, "How long ago did it happen?"

"Not more than two and a half, maybe three hours." The officer was looking through his paper work. "Yeah, CSI cleared out about twenty minutes ago."

"Is this his truck?" asked Agent Blackwell, pointing to the Ford.

"We don't know. We've run the plates and they're registered to an Austin Cole out of Jasper County, Texas. The registration in the truck checks out but no sign of him." The three agents stole a quick glance at each other. "Since we can't find him we're going to impound the vehicle for now. Honestly, we're pretty sure it's his though."

"Anyone get a tag number on the SUV?" ask Agent Birch.

"No," replied that officer. "Everyone we talked to said it just happened too fast. Most of the residents here are older, retired and don't have very good eyesight."

Rachael thought for a second as she scanned the subdivision. "Are there any security cameras around that you know of? Maybe something down the street in either direction? I mean, there's only one way out of this subdivision, right?"

"I know the convenience store about two blocks that way has a camera," the officer responded, pointing to the west. "There's also a car dealership just up the road that I'm sure has one," this time tilting his head to the east. "The house down there at the end of the street, the one with the blue shutters, had cameras installed but the homeowner didn't know how to operate it. The IT guys were supposed to come back out to take a look. I don't think they have yet."

"Thank you, officer," Rachael extended her hand to the policeman. The agents were walking to their car when she stopped and asked one last question of the patrolman. "Did anyone check that house?" she asked, pointing down the street to Cromwell's home.

"I don't think there was anyone home when we knocked."

Again, the agents thanked the officer and immediately began searching for video surveillance that might provide a tag and maybe a direction. *Crumb trail,* Rachael thought. They started by stopping at the house at the end of the street.

A small, elderly gentleman with a bald head filled with age spots shuffled his feet to answer the door. After Rachael identified herself and the other agents she was allowed inside to see if she could access the security footage. Several moments later she had managed to display the video of the event. The security system was elaborate enough that she was able to freeze and zoom making it fairly easy for her to get both license plate number and clear head shots of two of the suspects and one image of the victim. As the agents drove back by Cromwell's they stopped at the patrolman's vehicle and provided him with the plate number they had acquired then departed for the convenience store.

Within an hour the agents had determined that the Cadillac Escalade had headed west and had about a two hour head start. The agents started their trek west, stopping occasionally at venues which the agents thought may provide more video evidence of time and direction. Meanwhile, the photos of the perpetrators were sent to NSA headquarters for identification. The Facial Recognition Software made short work of the identification.

Rachael's phone rang. "Yes." It was Agent Greg Benton.

"Hey, Rachael. We've got a positive on one of the two suspects in the kidnapping and a likely on the other. The tall, muscular guy as you described him is Samir Halimi, a well-known mercenary currently thought to be in the employ of an arms dealer from Morocco: Medhi El Azzouz. We think the other guy is Farid Tsouli, also a gun for hire. His forte is as a sniper. Basically, these are some bad guys."

"Can you send me agency photos for all three men?"

"Sure; you'll have them in about 10 minutes," Greg said as he'd already begun the process.

"Any intel as to why they're here?"

"No, but we're working on it," he responded. "I'll let you know as soon as something comes through. Anything else?" asked the desk agent.

"Not right now. Thanks, Greg." Rachael hung up.

As promised, the photos were emailed to her phone within 10 minutes and she had a clear image of all three suspects but nothing on the victim. They had been driving for several hours, traveled no more than forty five miles, but had stopped at nine different small businesses collecting data and following the video trail that the kidnappers had unknowingly left behind.

It was well past dark, almost 10:00 p.m. They had

not eaten since takeout just after leaving the airport earlier that afternoon. The collective decision was to stop briefly, have a small meal then get back on the trail. The challenge was going to be finding something still open and serving food at this late hour.

Their very next stop was a combination gas station and restaurant that advertised the best home cooking in the south. The team thought it sounded perfect and hoped they weren't arriving too late. They entered through the restaurant door which still displayed the open sign and surveyed the almost empty dining area. They were greeted by a small, wide, older woman with a slight limp, grey-white hair and smile the size of the three menus she was carrying.

"Welcome," she said, reaching over for three place servings wrapped in cloth napkins. "Where would you like to sit?"

"Anywhere is fine," replied Agent Birch who was then led to a booth near the front of the dining room. Their host explained that the kitchen was in the process of closing down so the full menu was unavailable but they still had a lot from the buffet if they'd like. All three ordered from the buffet with coffee and a glass of water.

Twenty minutes later the agents were paying and ready to leave when Agent Harris asked to see the manager of the station. He was then able to view the security footage from between the hours of 2:00 and 5:00 p.m. They played the video several times and arrived at the same conclusion. Clearly, the captors had not come this far.

They had to have turned, Rachael thought. Try as she may, she couldn't remember how many turnoffs there were, if any, between here and their last stop. "We're going to have to back track and look for any roads that turn off along the way." Rachael opened her door and slid in while Harris tossed the keys to Blackwell who caught them cleanly and in stride.

"Your turn." Harris made the passenger side door and was on his way into his seat.

"Wondered what took you so long." Blackwell smiled as he walked around the front of the Crown Victoria and took over as driver. They made a 180 out of the parking lot and began their slow tedious trek back along their previously traveled path.

Stomachs full, energy spent, and focus beginning to fail, the agents sat quietly as they drove the almost deserted road. Each looking out their respective windows, carefully hoping to find a turn that might lead them to their targets, Harris finally found one turn to the right that they decided to investigate. It was a paved road but not far from the highway turned into a poorly maintained gravel road which looked more like a driveway than a county road, so they turned around at the first chance they got.

Beginning to think it best they find a hotel and start fresh in the morning, Blackwell was just about to speak up when Rachael tapped the back of his head rest.

"Slow down!" she almost screamed as Blackwell followed her instructions. "Did you guys see that?" she asked, pointing to the left, out into the darkness. The car was now almost at a dead stop.

"What is that?" Blackwell strained to make out what was so well hidden by deep over growth and obscurity of nightfall. Harris leaned forward so that he could see past Blackwell but he too was unable to make anything out.

"That looks like some kind of old, abandoned industrial park." Rachael seemed to be counting. "Looks like there may be, what, five or six roof tops that I can make out."

"Might make a perfect place to hide out," suggested Agent Harris. He turned to Rachael. "If there's someone in there, I think we need to move on then come back and take a closer look on foot." Looking at Blackwell he asked, "What do you think?

"We'll go on up the road, turn around and park a half block away," he replied, stepping on the gas. Two minutes later the three agents were on foot in shoulder high weed grass and half grown trees all wearing their best office attire. No one complained. They made their way through some overgrowth that looked as though it had recently been driven over.

Oh yeah! They're here! Rachael reached back and pulled her weapon out of its holster with her right hand while signaling Agents Harris and Blackwell to do the same. She pointed at the pressed-down grass with automobile tire spacing and then pointed forward. They stooped down a bit, began to spread out but stayed within eyesight of each other as they made their way further back into the industrial park.

What was once concrete drives were now riddled with cracks filled with high grass, weed and shrub, but even in the darkness the tracks from the SUVs were clearly evident. They followed the tracks around one building, then the next, and then the next until finally they saw the SUV sitting just outside the door to another old warehouse.

Rachael didn't want to get any closer. These guys were well known mercenaries and were most likely heavily armed. *If they're inside*, thought Rachael, *we're going to need a lot of backup*. She motioned the other two agents back and they retraced their steps until they were out of earshot and couldn't be seen from the warehouse.

"I'm not really sure what to do here." Rachael looked at the other two agents as though they would have the answers. Neither spoke up. "I couldn't see the plate clearly, but that was definitely the SUV that snatched Cole." She paused.

"Well, if he's in there, we really don't want to make things worse by raiding the place," suggested Blackwell. "I think we wait them out; see where they're headed."

"Sounds good to me," said Harris. "Too late to call HQ and get orders."

Rachael paced slowly but didn't offer a counter proposal. Finally she put her hands on her hips, looked over at the industrial park and then turned to the agents. "I don't get it. We're watching Cromwell. Looking for a Chinese national, oh yeah, who turns out to be a spy, who leads us to Moroccan arms dealers, who've kidnapped a 'nobody' from Texas, who for some reason has some kind of business with Cromwell." She took a long breath. Looked back at the warehouse. "How does this happen? What are these people into? And who is Austin Cole?"

CHAPTER SIXTEEN

Tuesday, June 16th, 2:30 a.m.:
Outside Houston, Texas

With his head still pounding from the beating he'd taken hours earlier, the application of the alcohol, hydrogen peroxide and Neosporin didn't seem to be as painful as Austin had expected. Yi Fun had gently washed away the blood from his face and neck and had bandaged each wound. With nothing else to do, conversation seemed to be their only distraction.

"So, how did you come to be kidnapped by these men?" she asked while leaning back against the wall.

"I don't understand it. I just drove down here trying to find my brother," he replied, his head beginning to fall back against the wall. "I thought he may have come to see this Cromwell guy so I went to his house. Next thing you know, I'm in an SUV with some big uglies and a hood over my face." His speech was starting to slow and his eyelids, while less swollen, were still quite heavy. "What about you?"

"I am looking for my brother as well." She started to explain. "He is a post-graduate student at MIT. He has been missing for almost 4 weeks now. The only lead that I had was an address which led me to the Cromwell residence." Austin began to perk up a bit as she continued. "When I arrived I discovered the men who took you were watching the house so I began watching them while planning how I would get into the Cromwell home without being detected. They captured you before I had the opportunity to make my attempt. After they captured you, rather than break into the home I decided to follow them in the hope that they may lead me to my brother."

Still somewhat hazy Austin said, "Well, I'm glad you made that choice, otherwise things could have gotten real ugly." He thought for a moment about what she had said. "You know, that can't be a coincidence." Austin slightly shook his head. "We're both looking for our brothers and their trails led us here." Austin paused. "What do our brothers have in common that would get them involved with these guys?"

"I do not know. My brother was doing post-grad-uate work in plasma physics. What does your brother do?" she asked, trying to find the common link other than Cromwell.

"He's a welder. He does construction." He paused again. "I just don't get it." His speech began to slur and he was beginning to get so tired it was difficult to keep his eyes open. He let his eyes close, took a breath then asked, "So why did you rescue me?"

"With you having been inside the warehouse, I thought you may have seen my brother or perhaps you knew where or why he was taken." She stretched out her legs as though she were about to lie down. "When I saw the hood over your head it was clear you'd seen nothing." She looked Austin in the eyes. "Why do you think they took you? Do they think you know something or have something?"

"This one guy, small guy, lots of cologne, kept asking about something called EMPTEC." Austin again nodded. "He seemed to think I knew where it is."

"What is EMPTEC and why would he think you know where it is?"

"Well, first I don't have a clue where it is and I'm not really sure I know what it is," replied Austin, lifting his right knee slightly to get better support. "It's got something to do with an old experiment that apparently blew up when the shuttle disintegrated on re-entry. My brother was looking into it when he disappeared. It was kind of a hobby of his. I thought he came to see Cromwell because he thought Cromwell was somehow involved."

For a few moments there was deafening silence then Austin spoke up. "So how did you do that?"

"Do what?" asked Yi Fun.

"Go all stealthy, kung-fu fighter and get me out of there. You're obviously not your average 'made-in-the-USA' kind of girl." Austin waited for her response.

Yi Fun deliberated carefully before she answered, unsure if she should divulge her secret. Deciding at this point it may not matter, she replied, "I am Kao Yi Fun. I am an agent of the Chinese Ministry of State Security. You can call me Yi Fun."

"What? Like a secret agent or something?"

Yi Fun smiled, then continued, "When I discovered my brother was missing I came to America without permission from my government to try to find him."

"So, you could be in big trouble." Austin realized the price she may have paid. "I'll bet the U.S. is looking for you, too. Will you be able to go back home once you find your brother?"

"I do not know. It will be difficult and dangerous."

Austin could see that this was not a comforting subject. "So, subject change; do we have a plan?"

"Tonight we sleep until light. Then we try to find Mr. Cromwell." Again there was quiet except for the sounds of the crickets.

"You know," Austin started again, "One of my dad's friends used to work for NASA until about 1998 or 1999. He lives just a couple of hours from here. He was a NASA engineer. He may be able to help us figure this out."

Yi Fun seemed hesitant and didn't reply.

"Look, this stuff is way over my head. Cromwell is going to be there whether we go in the morning or later in the afternoon. Either way, we need to know what we're going to be asking about. We also need to be prepared for our friends to make another appearance."Yi Fun cautiously agreed and they decided to get some much needed sleep.

About an hour after first light Yi Fun had awakened and prepared for the drive while allowing Austin a few extra minutes of sleep before getting on their way. Once prepared, Austin was awakened and they started their short drive to Milburn, Texas, and the home of Stephen Daniels. They had only managed a few hours of sleep so Austin was thankful that Yi Fun was driving, especially with his head pounding the way it was. He took a couple of pills for pain and then provided the directions as Yi Fun drove.

The travel time was good, stopping only for a quick breakfast and several cups of coffee. They arrived at Mr. Daniels's home around 10:30 a.m. The driveway was long, narrow, rustic and created a feeling of mystery and magic by making a couple of small curves around tall, old trees on either side creating a canopy over the driveway. As the driveway ended it widened then opened up to display a beautiful, two-story brick home with steep-pitched roof and inviting entry complete with a mat at the door that said 'Welcome'.

Austin took the two steps up to the landing and pressed the doorbell twice. Moments later the door opened revealing a man who Austin knew to be in his late fifties. He was shorter than Austin but still in very good shape for a man of his age. The smile with which he greeted them was genuine and not unexpected as it was typical of each visit Austin and his father had made to visit his dad's old friend.

"Hello, Austin! How are you?" He stepped back invitingly. "Come on in."

"Hey, Mr. Daniels," said Austin as he and Yi Fun entered the home. "How have you been?"

"Just getting older," he replied with a hint of laughter. "Not a lot to keep me busy now that Louis finished school. You know, he's working as an intern in Washington now?" He led them into the den where through each large window was a perfect view of a massive, blue-green lake. "Have a seat," he said, as he fell back into his recliner. "So, who's your friend?"

"This is Kao Yi Fun," he replied. "She's a friend. We're both in a bit of trouble that we think you can help with."

"What's the story?"

Austin started to explain and when he got to the part involving Cromwell and NASA Mr. Daniels stopped him.

"Do either of you have a smart phone on you?"

"No," replied Austin. Yi Fun shook her head in the

negative as well.

"Good," Stephen said. "Why don't we take a walk outside? My wife is planting some flowers that I think you'd both like to see." He stood and led them through the double glass doors that led to a large, stone patio with stairs which took them down to a stained pier on the shore of the lake. Again, he scanned his surroundings then again began to speak. "It's not safe to talk inside. Hell, I'm not sure it's safe out here but I guess we'll find out. The government can turn your cell phones on without you knowing it, activate the microphones and listen in to any conversation they want to. If you have a smart anything then you aren't immune. Now, go on," he directed.

Austin explained everything that had happened and detailed their plans for later that day. "Where we need your help is this: I really don't understand this NASA stuff. I'm not sure what to ask Cromwell when we see him. I know he's somehow involved with our brothers' disappearances but don't know how. And what is EMPTEC?"

Mr. Daniels took a breath, pushed himself away from the railing on the pier then pulled himself back up to it, his face dimming a bit, then he folded his arms. "Well, I'll tell you this. I worked with Harold Cromwell for almost eight years and I just don't see him as being involved in anything nefarious." He looked at Yi Fun then to back to Austin. Holding his breath for a moment, he swung his head slowly to the left and then to the right. *He's obviously weighing his options on something* Austin thought. Mr. Daniels continued.

"I can get into a lot of trouble for breaching my NDA with NASA so if it sounds like I'm hee-hawing around some things it's because I'm trying to protect myself as well as you."

He leaned against the railings of the pier and looked out over the water as both Austin and Yi Fun moved in closer. The sky was a beautiful shade of blue and reflected perfectly on the lake water that was as smooth as glass. The area was quiet with a hint of a lawn mower and some birds or ducks but otherwise could be described as serene. After taking in the view for a few brief moments Mr. Daniels was ready to continue.

"Back in the late seventies there were several projects that we were working on, most of which were to develop laser technology and find ways to utilize the effects of electro-magnetic pulse, as well as defend against it. You can imagine what kind of problem that would be in space. We had made some good progress, too. A lot of those developments have made their way to consumers. By the mid-to-late eighties NASA had been given a new directive to develop space based technology that would all but prevent successful missile launches from anywhere by anyone."

Mr. Daniels stepped back, moved to the other side of the pier and sat down on a bench. Austin and Yi Fun turned and followed. Austin sat down on the bench next to him. Yi Fun remained standing and her gaze followed the shoreline and surrounding homes as if keeping watch.

"To meet the requirements we'd need newer, better engines that didn't have much need for chemicals that would have to be replenished. We'd need a way to make those engines impervious to EMP's. And I'm sure they'd need to add weapons. By the late nineties certain military groups had gotten involved and there were initiatives to combine the technologies of EMP, laser and new research into ion plasma engines and EMP Dampener Technology."

"Ok, I don't think I understood any of that. But what's all of that got to do with Nick?"

"By the time I retired most of the technology had been developed and tested. Hell, I'm pretty sure that in some cases it's even been used. I've got to believe, given how far the technology had come since I retired, that it had to be ready for testing in space, if it hadn't already begun!"

Austin looked at Yi Fun whose focus never left the shoreline except to occasionally glance at Austin, then to Mr. Daniels and back to the shoreline. "So you think that EMPTEC is the result of all that research and that it was on that shuttle when it exploded?"

"I think it's likely." Mr. Daniels stood. "I'll tell you this: If it was and any significant part of it made it to the ground intact a lot of really bad people are going to want to get their hands on it!"

Yi Fun looked at Austin, fascinated with both his deductive reasoning as well as his subtle yet direct style of interrogation. *Impressive for a cowboy,* she thought. Then she looked over at Mr. Daniels and decided to ask a question of her own.

"So why would these people need a young welder from Texas and a student from China to find what is surely by now a piece of rusted waste?"

"Well, let's see," started Mr. Daniels. "What is your brother a student of?"

"He is a student at MIT doing post-graduate work in applied plasma physics," she replied. When she heard herself say the word the answer was immediately obvious. "Oh. I see."

"Yes, I'm sure that his knowledge of plasma would certainly help someone find a way to identify missing components and possibly repair them." Mr. Daniels walked away from his two interrogators briefly then turned back toward them. "So, when you went in and rescued Austin you found no signs of your bother or Nick?"

"There was only one guard outside," Yi Fun explained. "The others had driven off in their second vehicle."

"I see, so they could still have them but at some other location." He was quiet again. "But, what I can't figure out is why they would need a welder all the way from Texas when they could find one anywhere they managed to end up."

It was now clear to Austin that they'd managed to get as much information from his dad's friend as he could give. He looked at Yi Fun who understood what he was thinking without having to hear him speak. He said it anyway. "Well, looks like we still have to pay Harold Cromwell a visit."

"You realize that those men will surely be there," Yi Fun pointed out. "The moment they see us they will come."

"We'll just need to be prepared," responded Austin, subtly raising his eyebrows and displaying what Yi Fun saw as a hint of a confident smile. Austin moved back toward the opposite railing on the pier, rested both forearms on the top and took a lingering look out at the water. "We'll figure out a way in so they won't see us. Mr. Cromwell is the key and we are going to get some answers."

Mr. Daniels had remained quiet, head turned downward, looking at his hands playing with a piece of pine straw he'd picked up from the yard on his way down. Raising his eyes, looking first at Austin then to Yi Fun, he inched over to Austin and touched him on his shoulder.

"How do you think they knew about a young student from half way across the country having some connection with Cromwell?" He looked over at Yi Fun.

"I do not know." Her answer was short and direct.

"My guess is that if they have the Cromwell home under surveillance, they also have his home bugged and they check his mail for correspondence." Again, he thought for a moment. "Cromwell is retired NASA. He may also have his phones tapped by the NSA or CIA or some agency. The real question is do either of these sides know the other is watching, or should I say listening?"

"We're going to have to be careful," said Austin. "We can't expose Yi Fun to any of the agencies."

"But you've got to deal with these arms dealers. You understand men like these aren't afraid to be aggressive?" He watched Austin's reaction carefully then added, "You're going to have to match their violence if you're going to make it through this. Subtle and under the radar won't be an option." This time he looked deep into Austin's eyes looking for evidence that he completely understood what he was being told.

As if conceding something Austin said, "I get it." Then quickly giving Yi Fun a brief but cautious look of concern, he composed himself, looked directly at Mr. Daniels and said, "No more mister nice guy!"

Mr. Daniels smiled and gave a sigh. "Well, I think I

have something that can help. Follow me." Austin and Yi Fun followed closely behind Mr. Daniels whose pace had increased significantly as compared to the trip from the house to the pier. *Moves pretty good for an old guy,* thought Austin as he stepped off the pier into the lush green grass and began the walk up to the garage offset from his home.

Once inside the garage Mr. Daniels walked over to a wall-mounted storage cabinet, touched something on the right side then rotated the cabinet out, away from the wall, exposing a small doorway slightly larger than an ironing board. The doorway had no door knob and no apparent hinges. Yi Fun and Austin waited patiently, curiously as Mr. Daniels stepped over to the hinged corner of the cabinet and did something to the lower hinge. Instantly the ironing board door slid down and into the floor of the garage.

Austin and Yi Fun exchanged a look of shared surprise but didn't say a word. Instead, they followed their guide down the steep, narrow stairs to the hidden shelter waiting below. As his foot first touched the top stair Austin just couldn't help himself. "Your own little man cave!"

"You could say that," replied Mr. Daniels as he flipped the lights on illuminating the massive number of weapons and ammunition aligning each wall and on several multiple-shelved stands. There were hand guns of all models, autoloaders & revolvers mixed in with rifles like the AR-15, the Armalite M15A2 and the DSA SA58 tactical autoloader. There were shotguns from several eras as well as flintlock pistols. Every weapon looked like new and each were displayed as if in a high end gun store.

"Best man cave EVER!" Austin exclaimed scanning the room like a six year old going to his first comic book store. Yi Fun was equally impressed as both she and Austin browsed through the collection. Each picked up several of the handguns, carefully evaluating them then gently putting them back into their respective places.

Mr. Daniels waited as they seemed to touch every gun on display until finally he said "We're going to need the good stuff. The best handguns will be over here and except for two that I have in the very back the most efficient rifles are over there." He started pulling out a few of the handguns and matching extra loaded clips for each.

Austin, still in awe of the collection staged before him, rushed to the Glock 31, 357 automatic with the 17 shot magazine, but also spotted the Glock 17 and was immediately torn. Hesitant but for a moment, he decided to take both, looked for spare clips and went to the rifles.

Yi Fun had found her weapon of choice in the

Ruger P89. It was a 9mm with a 15 shot clip. *More shots is better but need something with punch,* she thought as again she scanned the remaining firearms. She spotted a 45 caliber autoloader and picked it up as well, rounded up extra clips and checked to see if they were filled. Of course, they were.

As she started toward some of the smaller firearms to her right she saw Mr. Daniels coming from the back of the unit carrying a DSA SA58 tactical autoloader with scope, several pins and three vests. "Hope we don't need these but better to be safe," he said handing one vest to Austin and then one to Yi Fun.

"What do you mean, 'we,' Mr. Daniels?" asked Austin.

"Well, the way I see it, you're going to need someone to cover you from outside if these guys show up and you're inside." He lifted his rifle a bit. "I'm pretty good with her from about 150 to 200 yards. If I can get the right vantage point we should be good."

"So, I'm not talking you out of this am I?"

"Nope. And I figure now is a good time to start calling me Stephen. And you're going to need a change of clothes; something more appropriate. We can check in the house. My son leaves some of his clothes here." He sized up Austin then said, "They'll probably fit."

Austin placed everything, including the vest he'd just been given, onto a table as if taking inventory.

Stephen followed suit. Yi Fun watched as Austin broke down the two Glocks, checked them thoroughly, and then reassembled them in moments. Again, she was impressed.

"Did I ask you what kind of work you do?" she asked Austin curiously awaiting his answer.

He continued his tasks while providing a simple, "No." He looked over at Stephen who returned his glance. "I'm a construction manager for a company out of Jasper, Texas." He tried on the vest, set the straps and returned it to the table.

"I see." Yi Fun picked up her vest and tried it on as well. All three stepped back from the table as if saying 'we're done'.

Mr. Daniels squeezed by Austin and headed to the stairs. "Y'all put everything in the car. I'm going to go break the news to the wife." He took the first step and added, "This isn't going to be pretty." He stopped just at the doorway and turned to Austin. "I'll bring you some clothes to change into." He then disappeared through the doorway and out into the garage.

Yi Fun and Austin shared another look then immediately started picking up all the equipment. As they started toward the stairs Austin noticed a pair of binoculars complete with a night vision function, fumbled around and placed them onto the pile already in his arms. Yi Fun was already at the top of the stairs as

FALLOUT

Austin started up. A few minutes later the trunk compartment of Yi Fun's 2015 Challenger was fully loaded
and the two were leaning against the fenders waiting
for Stephen's return.

They didn't have to wait long as Mr. Daniels, head
down and stride less than perky, came walking toward
the two carrying a large, dark colored duffle bag with
two straps and apparently completely filled. When
he got close to the Challenger, he tossed the clothes
over to Austin who quickly changed in the garage then
rushed back to the car where Stephen and Yi Fun had
already moved toward the doors.

"How did it go?" asked Austin even though he had a
pretty good idea based on Stephen's demeanor.

"She's not happy. Really hate to leave her like that."
He turned toward the garage and said, "Let me lock the
shop down and I'll be right with you." He stopped for a
second and handed the duffle bag to Austin. "Thought
this could be useful. Haven't used this in years but I
think it still works." He walked away then disappeared
into the garage.

"You think he will be ok?" asked Yi Fun.

"He'll do just fine; besides we need a spotter and a
long shot. He's done it before and we really don't have
a choice." He gazed back toward the garage for a moment then turned back to the car. "If it's all the same
with you, I'll drive on the way out. It'll just be quicker

if I don't have to give directions."

Yi Fun thought this request interesting as having driven here herself, she was well aware of the way back to Mr. Cromwell's. Still, she complied. "That's fine," she said and opened the door to the passenger side and waited for Mr. Daniels. She watched him as he shut the outer garage door and walked to the car. "Would you prefer to sit in the front seat?"

"No. I'll be fine in the back." He pushed the seat back forward and climbed into the back seat without hesitation. Soon, Yi Fun was in her seat, door closed and buckled up. Austin had already started the car and started to drive as the seat belt buckle clicked shut.

The driveway was as scenic on the way out as it was on the way in and the shade as thick even though the sun was almost directly above. The umbrella of tree limbs and leaves allowed only enough June sunlight through to provide clear view of where you were going and let you know it was summer. Once they made it to the highway Stephen offered some ideas on their next moves.

"We need to do a little research on that subdivision before we go back. We probably need to find a computer. I think there's one of those coffee houses with computers you can pay to use in town. We could be there in about ten minutes."

"Sounds like a good idea." Austin looked over at Yi

Fun. "That ok with you?" She nodded her agreement. "You just tell me how to get there."

As promised the drive wasn't long at all and in minutes they were driving along a side street leading up to an old converted home. Parking was provided in the form of a gravel lot and there was a picket fence which lined both sides of the walkway leading to the entrance. The sign read Comp 'n Coffee. Austin pulled into the parking lot and backed the car up so that his tag would not be easily seen, then started to open his door.

"Probably best you let me go in," recommended Stephen. "We know the NSA is looking for her and by now I'm sure they know who you are. Your faces are going to be posted all over the internet and television." It made sense to both Yi Fun and Austin so Yi Fun opened the door and allowed Mr. Daniels to exit.

He briskly walked up to the entrance then disappeared into the internet café. Austin and Yi Fun sat quietly waiting for Stephen's return. Yi Fun was carefully evaluating their environment and was wondering if Austin was doing the same. They were somewhat hidden by several other cars in the lot. They had clear line of sight to the side street from which they turned off and the more traveled street it intersected with. A tall, wooden, leaf-panel fence to their right blocked the view of the neighboring business and nothing behind them except a line of tall oak trees with galvanized posts stuck in the ground about every twelve feet and a triple wrapped galvanized wire running through holes in each.

Yi Fun stole a look at Austin who was alternating his focus between the rear view mirror and the side view mirror before checking the streets again. Just as Yi Fun started to look back to her side view she caught a glimpse of Mr. Daniels walking back to the car, several sheets of paper in hand. "Let's go," he said as he was ducking into the back seat. Austin put the car in gear having already started the engine and they were on their way to Houston and a date with Mr. Cromwell.

CHAPTER SEVENTEEN

Tuesday, June 16th, 3:18 a.m.:
Outside Houston, Texas

The two SUVs slowly made their way out of the industrial park, carefully inching their way to the main road which remained lifeless and deserted. The headlamps from the vehicles made it seem as though the sun was shining on the hard black top of the paved highway and was a welcome change of scenery for the four men once they finally made their turn and raced off.

Seeing that their targets were preparing to leave, the three NSA agents had rushed back to their parked car, loaded up and prepared to follow. The black Crown Vic blended in well with the thick over growth and the SUVs never seemed to notice as they sped by them. Agent Harris waited a small amount of time to allow the subjects to get far enough ahead that they wouldn't see their headlamps as they entered onto the highway. As soon as they made the first shallow curve of the highway Agent Harris pressed the gas, turned left and kicked in every bit of horsepower the engine had.

Once he caught sight of the tail lights he backed off

the gas and tried to remain a reasonable distance away. He would occasionally flip on a turn signal when he saw one of the vehicles begin to enter a curve along the highway. If they were watching their rear view they'd think the car was turning, lose sight of them in the curve, then a few minutes later more lights would appear. They'd never think they were being followed. At least that was the plan.

After about half an hour of this game it was clear to the three agents that their prey were heading back to the same subdivision where they had just twelve hours earlier kidnapped one Austin Cole. The same subdivision where OS231 was living. The subdivision which was now quickly approaching. Harris decided to get closer so that they could have clear sight of where the Moroccan's were expected to turn.

With the large number of streetlights lining the highway, as they closed in on the entrance to the subdivision Harris decided he could back off a bit yet stay close enough to still see the SUVs when they made their turn. The subtle way they made their turn indicated to Harris that they did not know they were being followed. The surprise was that the turn they made was actually into an adjoining subdivision called Hidden Valley just before Shady Acres Estates. It was one that the agents knew did not have access to the Cromwell residence without first re-entering the highway, going one block and then making the next left turn into Shady Acres Estates and on to Cromwell's street.

Acting as the turn was an insignificant one Harris drove past the turnoff and drove another mile on the straight-a-way all the while keeping a close look in his rear view. Agent Birch had completely turned around in her seat to keep watch in case the vehicles had tried to elude them. The black Cadillac's didn't return to the access.

"Park it over here on the right for a bit so we can keep an eye on the entrance just in case they're trying to wait us out," ordered Birch. Harris complied, backing his car into the parking spot at the end of a small gas station where they'd stopped earlier during their investigation the day before. Their view was unimpeded. Birch looked at her watch. *Still a few hours before Greg gets in.* "Guys, let's try to get some sleep," she suggested, knowing they were all tired having been up all night.

"Sounds good to me," replied Harris. "I'll take the first shift. I'll wake one of you in an hour unless something develops."

"Wake me first," said Blackwell. "I'm really not that tired. I may be too pumped to sleep."

When Rachael awoke she quickly glanced at her watch. "Seven thirty!" Agents Harris and Blackwell just smiled. "I'm going to call HQ." She pulled out her cell phone. The battery was all but dead. "Either of you have battery left on your phones?"

The agents looked at their phones but Harris spoke up first almost braggingly saying "I've had mine on my car charger all night. You can use it."

Rachael took the phone. "Thanks. You think your charger will work with my phone?"

"It's company issue. Pretty sure it will," Harris replied with a smile and reached back for her phone but never took his eyes off the street entrance. He then handed it to Blackwell to plug in. Rachael began dialing.

"Agent Benton," answered the voice at the other end of the call.

"Hi, Greg. It's Rachael."

"Hey, Rachael. I've been trying to call you all morning. Is something wrong with your phone?" he asked.

Embarrassingly she said, "It's dead. I didn't bring my charger."

"Why didn't you use one of the other guys'?"

"Greg!" Getting him back on track, and trying to avoid any more humiliation, she said, "Listen, you should be receiving a forensic report from Houston PD sometime this morning!"

Greg interrupted. "That's why I've been trying to call you. We've got it and you won't believe what we've found!" He was playing it for all the drama it was worth. "There's a security block on that Austin Cole fellow. Director Hughes is getting his files unlocked now. Don't know how long that's going to take."

Agent Birch went numb not sure of what to think about that or how it played into this whole investigation. *More immediate problem,* she thought. "Patch me through to Director Hughes."

"I can't," he retorted. "I told you he's on the phone now trying to get security override on Cole."

"I'll hold," she blurted. "Transfer me the second he hangs up! He's going to need to talk to me." Benton acknowledged and placed her on hold.

Meanwhile Blackwell and Harris were discussing whether they should change their location as they'd been sitting in the same spot for at least 4 hours. "It's possible they made us and they're waiting for our next move," said Blackwell, peering down the street now busy with traffic. Harris started looking for a smart place to relocate to. He saw a possible alley next to a dumpster about one quarter of a mile further down the highway.

"We could probably hide most of the car on the other side of that dumpster and even get out and stretch our legs if we wanted," he replied enthusiastically.

Harris wanted to talk to Birch first but she was still on hold for the director. "We'll wait until she gets off the phone. See what she thinks."

Several minutes later Rachael heard Benton's voice on the phone once again. "Rachael, he's still on the phone. Do you still want to hold?"

Angrily she responded, "No! I Don't!" She switched the phone to her other ear. "Ok, here's what you are going to do. Write down exactly what I'm about to tell you. When I hang up, you immediately take that note into the director's office and place it on the desk directly in front of him. Do you understand what you're going to do?" she asked.

"Yes." Benton carefully wrote everything she said from that point forward down on a notepad. Once the call ended he personally walked the note up the flight of stairs and over to the director's office. He knocked on the door but was ignored. Again, he knocked but this time with more emphasis and placed the note against the glass for the director to see. As expected, the director motioned Benton into his office but never took the headset away from his ear.

Benton walked over to the director's desk and just as Agent Birch had demanded, placed the note on the desk in front of Director Hughes then stepped away. The director scanned the note having never looked up at Benton after he'd walked in. Benton watched as he seemed to be reading the note again.

The director spoke into the headset, "Sir, I'm going

to have to call you back. I need you to get me that re-lease immediately. I have agents in the field currently shadowing several foreign nationals and now we have them all in one location. This 'lock' is a serious un-known variable for my people. If something happens and my people are injured as a result of this delay I'm going to hold you personally responsible." The direc-tor hung up the phone and picked up the note while Benton stood nearby. "Rachael?"

"Yes sir. She seemed intense and insisted on speak-ing with you immediately, sir."

"Is she still on hold?"

"No sir." Benton seemed a bit unsure of how to phrase his response. "She held for some time and not knowing how long you were going to be, we decided to leave the note and ask you to call her as soon as you could."

"Thank you," said the director. He again picked up his headset and began dialing the number Rachael had given Benton to write down on the note.

When the phone rang in Rachael's hand she recog-nized the number as the director's office and answered appropriately, "Sir."

"What have you got exactly?"

Rachael passed on the details of the night's events. "And currently we're watching the entrance from about one mile away. We haven't seen them come out so they must be parked or have a safe house of some kind in that subdivision that we don't know about." She paused for a moment waiting to see if the director may have orders or comments. When it was clear he was still waiting for her, she continued. "We didn't see any sign of the kidnapped Mr. Cole when they were loading their vehicles so we believe he is probably still inside the warehouse. His condition is unknown. We are concerned that the subjects are waiting for Mr. Cromwell to arrive home and...."

"I wouldn't worry about Mr. Cromwell," the director interrupted. "We've already had him moved to a safe house in Louisiana. They'll be waiting a long time."

"So should we go pick them up?" Birch asked.

"Here's the thing, Rachael. They must have been watching Cromwell's house for some time and they never approached him. Not that we're aware of, anyway. Then, suddenly out of nowhere this mysterious Mr. Cole arrives and twenty minutes later they have him in an SUV and are speeding off to a deserted warehouse."

"I see. They're not after Cromwell" Agent Birch's eyes widened. "They're after someone who's looking for Cromwell!"

"Exactly," the director replied. "We still don't know who this Mr. Cole is. I hope to have his file unlocked by late this afternoon. Meanwhile, I think one of you should try to find where the subjects have squatted and another should find a secluded yet very good view of the Cromwell home. I'll let you know if anything comes of the Cole file. Otherwise, if they try to take someone from the Cromwell home, or even approach the home, move in. Meanwhile, I'll have some special surveillance equipment sent to you from somewhere local. You should get it in about an hour."

"Yes sir. Thanks." There was no 'goodbye'. Both Rachael and the director just hung up. Rachael told Blackwell and Harris what Director Hughes's instructions were. "Do you have any ideas or suggestions?"

"I think it would be best to wait for it to get dark but I don't think we have that luxury," offered Agent Blackwell. "You know, in a few hours it'll be rush hour. There'll be a lot of cars turning onto these two streets. Maybe we could blend in."

Agent Birch was the first to respond. "I don't think I'd expect too much traffic turning into Cromwell's street. Most of those people are retired. We may have to think of something else. Don't know enough about that neighborhood," she said as she turned her eyes toward the entrance they'd been watching.

"Only one way to find out," said Agent Harris. "I can do some recon, at least get a feel for what it looks like beyond that fancy entry."

"You can't just drive up in there," stated Birch.

"They'd spot this car instantly."

"Well, I was thinking we could drive on down to that dumpster like Tim was saying. I could get out, take my jacket off, roll up my sleeves, pull my shirt tail out and take a stroll down the sidewalk and meander right on by. You could drive down and pick me up after I've gotten a quarter of a mile or so on past it."

Rachael thought for a moment. It sounded like a good idea although she thought he'd still look out of place. "Ok. Here's what we're going to do. Let's drive down there. Sit for a bit. Maybe one of us could go get something to eat while the other two keep watch. When 'whoever' goes to get lunch they could also pick up something in a large brown paper bag, something that would look like groceries." Harris and Blackwell again exchanged a look. Rachael realized she needed to explain. "That way you could look like you had walked to the store to pick up a few things and were on your way back home. Not an uncommon occurrence for normal people," she said sarcastically.

Harris considered her proposal. "Makes sense." He started the car, put it in gear and pulled down the street. It turned out the dumpster was sitting in front of a shop that was undergoing renovation which meant no tenants to deal with. Just up the street and on the same side was a little hole-in-the-wall burger place that advertised the best barbeque in Texas. Agent Harris doubted it. They all agreed to get a simple burger and fries with coffee if they had it. If not then just a soft drink with lots of caffeine and Blackwell volunteered to make the trek.

By 1:30PM Agent Blackwell had returned, two brown bags in hand, neither the size of which Rachael had in mind, yet still useful. Twenty minutes later Harris had finished eating and decided it was time to begin his hike. He stepped out of the car while Blackwell also opened his door and walked around the front of the car to take his new position at the steering wheel. Just as they'd planned, Harris threw his dark blue blazer into the back seat into Rachael's waiting arms who instantly folded it then placed it neatly on the seat beside her.

With his bright white shirttail untucked and wrinkled and his shirt sleeves rolled up to beyond his elbows, Agent Harris took the two brown paper bags, each filled with the trash remains from their lunch to make them look full, and proceeded to cross the three lanes of traffic to the sidewalk across the street. After having maneuvered his way across, avoiding several cars, a garbage truck and a motorcycle, he started his casual stroll towards the grand entrance which proudly announced Hidden Valley Way.

How appropriate, he thought as he read the street sign, now only about a block away. The entry was a well-manicured, sculpted landscape with a divided entrance, one for entry the other for exit. There was an island in the center adorned with a variety of colored flowers and shrubs and a small lighthouse that stood proudly near the front. The entrance side was lined with an eight foot high, stained, wooden privacy fence. In front of the fencing were small, rounded, green hedges that followed the long path of the fence as it curved its way into the subdivision. High heavy trees provided a canopy over the road as it merged into a single, two-lane street just beyond the island entrance.

His once neatly pressed, bright white shirt was now covered with sweat beneath his chest and underarms. His collar was drenched as were his rolled up sleeves especially at the elbows. Slowing his pace a bit as he passed in front of the lighthouse, he took a longer look focusing deeper down Hidden Valley Way, but the landscaped shrubbery and tall thick trees blocked him from seeing any sign of the two SUVs or even a house for that matter except those directly near the front. Feeling pretty confident that the men in the SUVs also were unable to see him, Harris motioned for the other two agents to come and get him. Moments later, Agent Birch pulled up to the curb beside Harris who opened the door and got into the front passenger side seat, immediately turning the air conditioning vents directly on himself.

"Where's Blackwell?" he asked, reaching for a napkin left over from lunch and wiping the sweat from his forehead.

"He's doing some recon himself. He's taking another look at that subdivision layout that Cromwell's street is on." Harris nodded his acknowledgment. Rachael drove off and continued for about two blocks. "So, what did you see?"

In a frustrated tone, Agent Harris responded with a simple, "Nothing. Trees blocked everything. The street curves to the left and right then takes a sharp turn right. I think the street makes a circle."

Rachael turned left across two lanes and into a small shopping mall, made a 180 degree turn then pulled up to the main street and flipped on her turn signal. She patiently waited for a blue Smart car and a black, late model Challenger to pass by, then turned back on to the main road with a bit of a jilt and proceeded back to the dumpster where she parked as if they'd never left. They waited about fifteen minutes before they saw Agent Blackwell reappear on the sidewalk near the entrance to Shady Acres Estates. Moments later he was getting into the back seat.

"Anything?" asked Agent Birch.

"I couldn't go in very far," he replied. "I think there are three streets that turn off of Shady Acres Lane but I think Shady Acres Lane is really a loop." He brushed the sweat from his forehead with his shirt sleeve. "It's weird but I think there's a privacy fence all the way around that place. I could see one way at the back as I walked in."

"Could you see any homes that looked like they were empty?" asked Harris.

"I only saw two houses, one on the corner near me and the one on the corner on the opposite side of Cromwell's."

He seemed a bit frustrated. Of course they were all tired. They'd been up almost all night, had very little to eat and *at least one of these guys needs a change of clothes and a shower,* thought Rachael. "We're going to need a new plan. Somehow we have to get into both of those neighborhoods without being recognized." She paused for a moment then said, "We need another car."

Rachael picked up her now fully charged smart phone and started a search for car rentals nearby. She found one estimated to be 1.6 miles away from their current location which sounded just great to her. Blackwell was left at the dumpster to keep watch while Harris and Birch made the drive to secure another car. Twenty five minutes later Harris was pulling back into the lot and backing up beside the dumpster. Blackwell seemed relieved as he opened the door and plopped into the front seat.

"Where's Rachael?"

Harris smiled a bit then said, "Wait for it." His eyes volleyed between the Hidden Valley entrance to his left and the street to his right. Several travelers drove by, a small pickup with a missing bumper, a couple of late model Hondas, a silver Prius and a green Camaro. Again, Harris smiled. "There she is," he said as the two agents watched the silver Prius turn right onto Hidden Valley Way. They couldn't help but let out an audible laugh.

"Hope she doesn't have to get out of that and flash her badge," poked Blackwell. "No one would believe her!"

Harris shook his head. There were just too many agent/Prius jokes in his head.

Rachael and her silver Prius slowly followed the curvature of the shade covered drive into Hidden Valley. About one block up there was a sign with an arrow pointing to the right and another sign which read 'No Left Turn'. She turned right and carefully continued on her way. For a brief way there were only homes on the left side of the street but then there was a fairly sharp turn to the left and houses lined both sides of the street from that point on.

Realizing that Cromwell's home was just behind one of these houses on her right and beyond the privacy fence that separated the two subdivisions, she slowed.

She calculated that the best angle to see Cromwell's home would be from one of the first five or six houses. The first was one of the smallest of the six but had a variety of children's toys in the front yard and on the driveway side of the house. *Probably not making their base there,* thought Rachael as she saw the young mother standing in her open doorway with a baby in one arm and a small trike hanging from her other.

The next two houses had full driveways, one with a white Lexus and an older model Ford Ranger. The other house had two cars parked in the driveway and one on the curb nearing the boarder of the yard. There was a Jeep Cherokee parked closest to the garage and directly behind it a blue Altima with a dented rear passenger side door that looked as though it had been that way for some time. The car on the curb was an older Honda Civic which looked as though it was wearing a coat of primer.

Looking ahead, Rachael noted the two black Cadillac Escalades parked in the driveway of the fourth house. The house didn't look vacant at all and didn't stand out in any way but as she drove past the house she noticed what looked to be one of those realtor key boxes lying on the porch floor to the side of the stairs. *Interesting; they could have taken down the 'For Sale' signs, busted the lock box, and everyone would think they'd bought the place.*

Rachael continued her drive making the loop on

Hidden Valley Way until she had reached the entrance and the intersection with the highway. By this time, traffic had begun to pick up and her exit from Hidden Valley was delayed by numerous cars traveling in both directions and a few making the turn into the subdivision. Finally, she saw a clearing and took the opportunity, pressed the pedal to the floor and shot out into the east bound lane and toward Agents Harris and Blackwell.

She backed the Prius up next to the Crown Vic and rolled down the passenger side window as did Agent Blackwell.

"So, what did you find?" asked Blackwell.

"They're definitely in there. It's the fourth house on the right. From the second floor back rooms they should be able to see at least three sides of Cromwell's house without obstruction."

"That's why it took them a few minutes before they got here to grab Cole. They had to make it out of Hidden Valley, then on to Main Street, then into Shady Acres." Blackwell had it figured out.

"So basically, all we have to do is wait to see who turns in to Shady Acres then let the Moroccans go in after them. When they do, we've got them," responded Harris.

"I hope it's that easy," countered Rachael as she continued to keep watch on Hidden Valley. Picking up her cell phone she started dialing. "I'm going see if we can find out everything the agency has on that house and see if they've found anything more on the Moroccans or Cole."

Again, Agent Greg Benton answered. "Benton."

"Hi Greg. Anything new on Cole yet?"

"No, but I see the director is back on the phone. I guess he's still pushing," he replied.

"Alright, let me know ASAP. Listen, I've got something else I need you to look into. I'm going to give you an address here and I need to know everything we can get on it and I need it within the next couple of hours. Also, I'm going to text you two license plate numbers from the SUVs we've been tracking. Run them and let me know everything you can find out about them."

"Sure. Do you want some fries with that?" Benton asked in his most sarcastic tone while already running the plates.

"No," she quickly replied. "But I think Harris could use a change of clothes if you can help with that."

"I don't think that's my department," he responded. His smile suddenly disappeared. "Hey! Hold on a minute." He paused then made a few audible mouse clicks which Rachael could clearly hear through her phone. "I just got a hit on those plates. You're not going to believe this. Those SUVs are leased by the Armenian Consulate."

CHAPTER EIGHTEEN

Tuesday, June 16th, 7:00 a.m.:
Suburb of Houston, Texas

It had been a fairly quiet night once El Azzouz and his men had reached the safe house. They managed to get some sleep while the other two men who'd been waiting at the home were maintaining surveillance on the Cromwell place. El Azzouz had ordered Samir Halimi to take over surveillance around seven o'clock in the morning to give the other two men some time to get some rest. Both men started down the hall to the second bed room on the upper level to sleep but were stopped by El Azzouz. Meanwhile, Younes El Aroud had slept all night and was well rested, back on the job of monitoring all of the listening devices they'd managed to plant in Cromwell's home, but there'd been no activity at all on any front.

Farid Tsouli had been tasked with cooking breakfast which was no small task as there were seven people to feed including the captive student of physics. While Tsouli was cooking downstairs in the kitchen, Samir was upstairs keeping a close eye on the home of Mr. Cromwell, not wanting to incur the wrath of El

Azzouz again so soon. The upstairs bedroom window which faced the residence was the perfect location for observing the activities from the street to the garage to the front door of Mr. Cromwell's. *When he shows up,* thought Samir, *we'll definitely see him.*

As Samir peered through the half open curtains of the master bedroom, surrounded by complex recording and monitoring devices and an assortment of firearms fully loaded and staged where they could be utilized in an instant, he could hear El Azzouz talking with the two men who'd been left to keep watch while they had been interrogating Mr. Cole.

"What time did they arrive?" asked El Azzouz.

"It was around five o'clock. A policeman was there with a wrecker to take away the truck," replied a nervous voice.

El Azzouz came back with, "How long did they stay?"

"They did not stay very long. When they left they went to one of the houses on the end of the street. They stayed there for about an hour, maybe less."

"Could you tell what direction they went when they left?"

"No sir. I could not. The homes and trees block my view for both directions. The policeman and wrecker left just before them.

El Azzouz started to walk away down the hall then

stopped with one more question. "Did anyone enter the Cromwell home?"

"No sir. The police knocked on the door but left when there was no answer."

Samir could hear footsteps leaving in both directions away from his post. It sounded as though someone went down stairs while the others continued down the hallway to the second bedroom. The home they'd chosen for their hideout was a tall, narrow but long two-story home with a small front porch and a steep slanting roof that seemed to only slope for any significant distance on one side. The back side of the home had a shorter roof and tall flat vertical wall which allowed for the upstairs bedrooms to have a taller roof line and place all of the closet space on the sloped side of the house. The two bedrooms were joined by a large bath with two entries, one from the hall and one from the larger bedroom.

By now, the enticing scent of freshly cooked eggs had permeated the air having even reached the second floor bedroom. Simir was hopeful someone would bring him a plate as he, too, had not eaten in over eighteen hours. As if his prayers had been answered, only moments later Tsouli walked in holding a full plate and a cup full of coffee which he placed on the small nightstand table which had been moved next to the window Simir was assigned to stand watch. Without saying a word Tsouli turned and left the room.

The house also came with a full basement which could be reached by stairway off the back of the kitchen near a doorway which led out onto a patio and into the back yard. The basement had the single access point from the first floor just off the kitchen. The large basement had car access through two large doors at the end, a center personal access door and four long windows along the back that were only about eight inches tall located near the roof line of the basement. The windows allowed some light in but while they could roll open there was not enough of an opening to enable access or exit. Tsouli's next delivery was down those stairs and into the mildew laden enclosure to deliver another meal.

A large portion of the basement had been transformed into what one might call a laboratory or workshop. There was electrical equipment, gauges, monitors, wires and cases of all kinds. Over to one side there was an acetylene-welding setup and an assortment of gloves, helmets and welding wire. All of the florescent lights were on as well as a bench light at a work station located against a wall at the far end of the basement. The brown, oil-stained work bench housed a small vice, several clamps, numerous rolls of wire in various gauge sizes and color codes, a soldering iron and solder wire.

Sitting on a stool, slumped over the table, leaning in

toward the bench light, was a smallish, dark-haired young man wearing magnifying goggles and holding some small needle-nose pliers in one hand and a strand of wire in the other. The musky scent of the gloomy, spider webbed basement had been overcome by the more potent odor of melting solder mixed with sweat and dust.

Farid Tsouli quietly walked up to the busy work bench apparently without disturbing the young man at the table. He waited for a moment for the smoke from the soldering to dissipate, then using the hand holding the glass of water, gently tapped the sweat covered worker on the shoulder. The Asian plasma physics student turned his head, looked over his shoulder and saw Tsouli holding a plate of food and a welcomed glass of water. He quickly cleared an area of the bench so that Tsouli could put the plate down and he took the glass of water directly to his lips.

"El Azzouz is eating. I heard him say when he was done he was going to come down and talk to you." Tsouli said nothing else, just turned and left to go back upstairs.

"Thanks," Yi Szun said without even looking at the departing Tsouli.

Yi Szun ate quickly but left no scraps. He wanted to be back at work before El Azzouz's visit. Once he was done eating he placed the plate on a barrel located off to the right of the bench, took another drink of the water and put the glass down just out of arm's reach. He then picked up the soldering iron and wire and went back to work sending streams of grey smoke floating upward and disappearing into the darkness above the fluorescent fixtures.

The soldering he was doing was on a board inside a container that was not unlike a large cell flash light. There was a handle on the top section which was lying off to the side and what would have been the lamp area was now more horizontal and housed some type of indicator that looked similar to an old Geiger counter. There were wires running from the top section into a board located in the bottom section that looked as though they came from a computer complete with male and female connection ports. Yi Szun was working on providing the phased power that the unit would need in order to operate correctly when El Azzouz approached from behind.

"How is your work progressing?" he asked without social convention.

Yi Szun nervously put down the wire and soldering iron then turned to face El Azzouz, as he had learned not to do so would be an act of disrespect, something El Azzouz responded negatively to. "Another few hours and it should be ready for testing."

"And, how will you test this?"

"Well, I will need either an EMP emitter or high

temperature plasma ejector and something made of the same metal as that which we are searching for. And it will need to be laced with trace levels of exposed plasma photons in order to get an accurate reaction," replied the uneasy captive.

"So where will we acquire these things?" asked El Azzouz, looking around the dingy basement.

"Most could be found at any college in the engineering labs and some laser research facilities," Yi Szun replied.

El Azzouz, arms crossed, stepped slowly toward the anxious young student then suddenly slapped Yi Szun across his left cheek leaving a bright rose-red imprint on his face. Yi Szun instinctively turned his head and grasped his cheek. El Azzouz's eyes followed.

"And how many laser research facilities are you aware of here? And how do you expect us to get those items?" El Azzouz paused then stepped back. He took in a deep breath then slowly let it out. Changing his tone he said, "You see? Now you have made me angry." He wiped his hand on his pants then crossed his arms again. "I do not wish to be like this. You will finish your project by tonight. Soon we will know the general location and you will have your opportunity to test your device then." He turned and took a few steps until he reached the stairs. "My hope for you is that the test is successful." He walked up the stairs and disappeared through the door at the top.

CHAPTER NINETEEN

Tuesday, June 16th,
5:30 p.m. local time thru 12:30 a.m.
Wednesday, June 17th

It had been a two hour drive with little conversation. Stephen was in the back seat going through all the maps and notes he'd printed out at the coffee shop. Austin and Yi Fun seemed too focused to talk, each seemingly lost in separate worlds. Just as they were approaching Shady Acres Estates a subtle smile brushed across Austin's face and the car slowed slightly as he looked into the rear view mirror. Yi Fun noticed the change and glanced at Austin who was still exhibiting his private smirk.

"Why are you smiling?" asked Yi Fun.

"Our NSA friends are here! That black Crown Vic we just passed had a different driver but was definitely the same car that paid me a visit back in Texas just after my brother disappeared. Come to think of it, one of the photos he showed me was of a young Asian man. Hmm. May have been your brother." He kept driving and continued on past the entrance to Shady Acres. "The guy in the passenger side identified himself as an NSA Agent."

Mr. Daniels raised his head from the mass of paper strewn across the back seat of the Challenger. "That means they know we're here. That or they're also watching Cromwell."

"Or both," added Austin. "Doesn't change what we've got to do." Austin looked over at Yi Fun. "You agree?" She nodded.

Austin drove the Challenger slowly by a small, brick, three story office building on the left and a five shop strip mall located just beyond the entrance to Shady Acres Estates. Just as Stephen had mapped it out, Austin took the first left turn and followed it around behind Shady Acres. They circled around the subdivision, and just as Stephen had expected based on his maps, there was no vantage point from which to get line of sight with Cromwell's home.

Stephen then suggested that they find a drive through and then park the car and eat while they weigh their plans. After getting their meals, Austin backed the Challenger into a parking spot while Yi Fun started distributing the food. Stephen apparently had already come up with their next move. Stephen sucked on the straw of his drink then folded open his sandwich and took a large bite and made quick work of the burger and fries then leaned back into the seat and took a deep, lazy breath.

Austin had managed to park so that the car was

facing the curve near the Shady Acres Estates entrance which he could not see from his current location but he did have an idea. "Stephen, do you see that office building down there on the right?"

"Sure. Why?" asked Stephen.

"It looks like it's located almost right up against the privacy fence at the edge of Shady Acres." Austin's eyes seemed to scan the other buildings and the landscaping around them. "I know we can't drive through and recon without everyone seeing. But if there was a way to get into that office building, at least to the second floor, higher if possible, we'd be able to see if there's a way in and if there is a good place for you to set up for cover."

"I see what you mean," acknowledged Stephen. "Why don't you drop me off and I'll take a look."

"Did you see the sign out at the street?" asked Austin. "You may look a bit out of place." Austin looked over at Yi Fun. "You good with that?"

Yi Fun took a deep long look at the brick bordered, double-sided sign then smiled. "Yes," she replied.

"We'll drive you down and park in the little strip mall on the right. You can walk over from there." Austin finished his sandwich, placed the trash in the bag then all the bags into a trash can, started the car and pulled down near the dry cleaners, backed into a parking spot and let Yi Fun out. As Yi Fun walked toward the office building, Stephen read the sign now only a few yards away.

"Yep," Stephen said conceding Austin's point. "I definitely think she's better suited."

Austin smiled. "Unless you've unexpectedly developed a uterus over the years, you'd really draw a lot of unwanted attention at a women's clinic."

Yi Fun entered through one of the double glass doors leading to the lobby of the tall, rectangular office building. The front of the building was a series of tall, narrow windows tinted with a reflective coating. Yi Fun noted on the stroll toward the building that the side nearest her had the same style windows on the second and third floors but smaller, non-coated windows on the first. She assumed it was because of the close proximity of the strip mall nearby.

Upon entering the lobby of the clinic, immediately in front was a directory identifying all of the tenants and their respective specialties along with the suite numbers in which their services may be found. There were stairs to her immediate left which bent and curved as they ascended from one floor to the next. Stairs from the first floor to the second were on her left but Yi Fun could see that stairs to the third floor went from the second floor on the right side of the building and the lobby was open all the way to the ceiling.

Yi Fun turned to her left to make the climb to the

second floor and noticed that there were also elevators just a few meters behind the directory sign. *Still,* she thought, *the stairs will provide access to a better view.* As she approached the top stair and landing to the second floor she stepped close to the window on her left and peered intently toward Shady Acres Estates and specifically at Cromwell's house. Although there were trees lining the street she could see clearly enough to make out all the details that she needed. After making all the mental notes of what she'd seen, estimated distances, unusual topography and the arrangement of the entire subdivision she casually turned and started the trip down the stairway and out through the glass door she'd entered only a few moments earlier.

Walking back down the sidewalk in front of the strip mall she indifferently glanced at her surroundings, into the respective store front that she was passing and then to the street and then down to the Challenger still parked in the same spot awaiting her return. Just as she started to step off the curb to cross the parking lot to the waiting car, her gaze was captured by the passing black Crown Victoria which Austin had pointed out as they were arriving. She stopped in her tracts for a moment to see if the car was going to turn into the strip mall parking lot. She glanced at Austin who was clearly aware of her hesitance.

Once the car had passed by without making the

turn Yi Fun quickly made her way to the car and hastily got in. Austin had already started the car and had pulled forward as she opened the door. She was buckling her seatbelt just as the Challenger was turning out of the lot and out into traffic.

"Problem?" Austin asked as he stole a glance at Yi Fun.

"Only on the walk back," replied Yi Fun. "I saw the black car you pointed out pass by. It was definitely the same one that you saw earlier. It seems they have a different agenda."

"You get what we needed?" Austin asked, bringing the subject back to the immediate task at hand.

"Yes."

Austin looked in the rear view to confirm that he was not being followed by another car. "Let's find somewhere to rest up, make our plans and wait until dark."

Stephen suggested a small hotel perhaps six to ten miles away in case the NSA or 'Mr. Cologne' and his crew were hanging around. He did a quick search on his cell phone for hotels in the area and found just the place about twelve miles away and no turns. Austin had them there in fifteen minutes. It was agreed that Stephen would go in and get the room hoping to pay cash but if he had to secure with a credit card at least his would generate less attention than Austin or Yi Fun for those groups who like to spy on citizens' purchases.

Once they had all managed to move everything into their room, they agreed to start formulating their plan. Stephen laid out all the maps he'd been able to print out at the coffee shop earlier in the day. They were pretty detailed. They clearly showed the entrance to Shady Acres Estates and Shady Acres Circle as it made its way around the subdivision although it was in reality less a circle than a rectangle split down the horizontal center by Shady Acres Lane. From the aerial views it was clear there were houses lining either side of each road with the exception of the Shady Acres Circle as it enters the subdivision. That entire length was lined with nicely landscaped flowers and shrubs in front of and in between larger shade trees. Behind the trees, about ten feet was a six foot high privacy fence. *They're nothing if not consistent,* thought Austin as he studied the views.

Yi Fun stepped up to the table and pointed at the Cromwell residence on the map then let her finger drag back away from the home toward the back of the property. "There is a concrete channel that runs the entire width of the subdivision parallel to Shady Acres Lane." Her finger continued to drag first to the left of Cromwell's home over to the outer edge of the subdivision where it apparently went under Shady Acres Circle. She then started pulling her finger back to the other side retracing her path back to Cromwell's and then on to the circle again and under the privacy fence near the women's clinic she'd visited earlier.

"This channel continues outside the community and behind the office building I was in earlier," she said, leading their eyes with her index finger. "There must be a duct or bridge of some kind that goes under the fence and the street." She didn't stop. She again pointed at the canal's path. "It is lined on both sides with a privacy fence at most locations. The home adjoining Mr. Cromwell's at the rear has a privacy fence but the one next to it only has a chain link fence."

"That could be our way in without being seen," said Austin looking closer at the canal. "That's assuming there aren't a lot of street lights."

"I saw no light posts at the rear near the channel for any of the homes," Yi Fun reassured. "However, flood lights or porch lights may present a problem. We will not know who may have theirs on and we will be unable to anticipate when someone may decide to."

"We'll just have to be deal with that when and if it happens and expect it to happen," Austin responded.

"Another issue may be pets," offered Stephen. "If these people have dogs they'll get every light in the whole neighborhood turned on the second we set foot near those fences."

"I was unable to see all the homes but for the ones I

did see there were no indications that anyone had dogs. By 'indications' I refer to dog homes." The two men shared a look and a brief smile. "What?" asked Yi Fun "Did I say it wrong?"

Austin was subtle. "Only a little, but we liked it!" He continued, "Anyway, that's good, although indoor breeds can be pretty loud and love to stare out the windows. We'll just have to move quickly and deal with it if it happens."

"Did you see a good place for me to setup?" asked Stephen. "I don't want to be so close that I can't provide a wide sweep of cover in case we need it."

"Two homes down from Mr. Cromwell's," Yi Fun again pointed to the aerial. "This home has what I think you refer to as a tree house, although there is no tree."

"So it's free standing?" asked Austin. "Was it higher than the top of the fence and how close to the fence is it? I mean the fence on that side of the canal."

"Mr. Daniels will be well above the top of the fence and should have an unobstructed 180° view and the free standing tree house is very close to the fence at the back of the yard that it is in."

"Seems like the perfect place to roost." Grasping his right, upper thigh he said, "If these old joints will let me climb the ladder that is!" He smiled for effect and Yi Fun and Austin shared a grin.

"We'll wait until we're sure he's gone to bed and

fallen asleep before we make the move." Austin paused for a moment, then took a sip of beer that was now warm, having been ignored all during the conversation. "Ok. So we now know when, where and how. Now let's talk about the party crashers. It only took about ten minutes for Mr. Too-much-cologne's men to load up, crank up and drive over to Cromwell's to bag me."

"So obviously they were waiting somewhere close by and it had to be someplace that they had a pretty good view of the place." Stephen was stating the obvious.

"And I don't think they were in this subdivision. When I first saw them they were almost on two wheels turning on to Shady Acres Lane leaning hard to the left. That would be my left. Anyway, they were clearly coming from the highway."

"They could not have been observing the Cromwell home from anywhere around the women's clinic. They would not have been able to see clearly enough that you had stopped." Yi Fun paused. "Unless they guessed."

"They didn't guess," said Austin. "That leaves the neighborhood next door." Austin pointed at Hidden Valley. "Stephen, once you get in place you're going to need to have eyes on any home or structure that those guys could be watching from." Stephen nodded.

The next five hours were spent preparing weapons,

organizing the flashlights, knives, wire cutters and some items of preference for each. All three had black back packs that they could put most of what they needed into. Stephen put the maps and aerial shots in his back pack. As the time arrived each one changed into darker clothing. Yi Fun was already wearing her gear but Stephen had to go purchase some for Austin.

As the time approached, the three stood together around the table, each picking up their weapons of choice and stowing them in the back of the pants waist line, strapped to their calves or around their thighs. Yi Fun noticed that Austin had placed duct tape around a knife shroud and had Stephen tape it to his bare back just between his shoulder blades. While the handle was protruding slightly through the black pullover it really wasn't going to matter unless he was captured.

By 11:30 they were loading into the Challenger and by 11:45 they were parked in a dead-end alley near the back of the women's clinic. The trunk was raised as they got out of the car and grabbed their respective back packs. Together, the three walked to the trunk and pulled out one long gun that each had picked out when at Stephen's. There was also a large duffle bag which Stephen pulled out just before he quietly shut the trunk lid.

"I brought a little something that I thought we might need," he said as he opened the bag and pulled out a large, brown box. He placed the box on the table and slid the bag off to the left. He unfolded the top flaps of the box then reached in and pulled out a single set of head phones with an integral microphone all attached to a small battery unit with a hook. He placed the head phones over his head and strapped the battery to his belt. Before placing the headphones over his ears he again reached into the box and pulled out two ear buds and twin lapel microphones and handed one each to Austin and Yi Fun.

As they accepted the apparatus Stephen pointed to the ear bud. "There's a small battery in each of these. They're fully charged now but keep in mind that they don't have a long battery life. I recommend we test them now, then turn them off and don't use them again until we're all in place."

"They only last about forty minutes or so right?" asked Austin as he looked closely at the pin before he placed it on his shirt.

"The ear buds last about an hour, maybe an hour and a half," explained Stephen, "but the microphones will only make it about forty-five if you don't use them too much." He placed the headphones over his ears. "Now, the way they work is…"

"To use the microphone," Austin interrupted, "you press on the ear bud, like a toggle switch on a radio?" He was telling more than asking even though it sounded like a question.

"Well, yes. You lightly press the ear bud to talk. You press it twice to turn it off. As for the microphone, you press it against your chest pretty hard to turn it on and off."

Yi Fun was carefully listening, all the while placing the microphone on her shirt and the ear bud into her left ear. It was clear to Austin that this was a familiar toy for her. "So what is the range of this device?" asked Yi Fun fully expecting Austin to respond before Stephen.

"Without high frequency interference, maybe two hundred fifty yards." Realizing he was talking to a Chinese agent, Stephen rephrased "Ah, about 228 meters."

"Alright, we know the plan," Austin said as he turned and started walking toward the nearby canal. "We'll give you about five minutes to get into place and set up. We'll turn on the buds in about four so let us know we're clear."

Climbing over a railing on a small walkway that crossed the canal, Austin stooped to the bottom of the bridge over-hang and lowered himself as far as he could, then let himself drop to the concrete below. Yi Fun and Stephen began dropping the backpacks and weapons down to Austin who quickly placed them to one side in the shadows safely out of the way of the others as they descended. Stephen was next in line as Yi Fun would be able to help from the top and Austin would help from the bottom. Once Stephen make it down Yi Fun followed Austin's lead and seconds later was standing on the canal floor and looking for weapons.

"Ok, we go silent from here," directed Austin looking at Stephen, "until we hear from Stephen that he's in place and it's clear." After nodding acknowledgements they began their walk to the bridge over the canal at Shady Acres Circle. Just before starting under the bridge Austin had one last thought, "Nobody gets hurt, right?" Both Stephen and Yi Fun nodded in agreement but as Stephen turned to proceed alone he stopped.

"Austin, I hear what you're saying and I understand why," Stephen said as diplomatically as he could, "but these men are not going to be thinking that way. They may just make it impossible for you to keep that promise." He looked at Austin one last time before he walked away. "I'm just saying, you better be prepared to do what you have to do." He disappeared into the shadows under the bridge as Yi Fun looked inquisitively at Austin.

Austin and Yi Fun watched Stephen reappear in the dimly lit canal in the opening on the other side of the bridge splitting the shadows falling from between the two fences which lined the canal. Walking slowly, and with both hands full, Austin figured it might take him a bit longer than five minutes to get set up. He kept a close eye on his watch waiting until the full four minutes he'd promised were up then he and Yi Fun turned the ear buds on.

"Can you hear me?" was the first thing Austin heard. Stephen followed his question with, "I'm on site and setup if you're listening."

Austin lightly pressed his ear bud. "Roger that." He looked at Yi Fun. "We're going in." He turned and led the way under the bridge and started counting the corner posts that indicated the end of one yard and the beginning of the next. Yi Fun kept close behind and maintained the pace established by Austin which was better described as a rapid walk than a run. Finally, they came upon the nearest corner of the Cromwell back yard. *Still no dogs barking. That's good,* thought Austin as he climbed up the wall of the canal and stepped over to the fence. He started to reach down and give Yi Fun a helping hand but when he turned she was already behind him awaiting his next move.

Austin started scanning the fence for a vulnerable spot that would be the most effective way in when he saw a small area about ten feet ahead where apparently there were two boards loose at the bottom. He looked Yi Fun in the eyes, pointed at the loose boards then started moving in. He worked his way carefully over to the boards to evaluate just how loose they were.

While holding on to the nearest post he reached down to tug on the bottom of the first board hidden from the moonlight by the shade. It pulled out about an arm's length as did the second one essentially creating the perfect access point for them to get through.

It seemed rather fortuitous that there were no security lights near the back of any of the yards in the neighborhood. To Austin, as he gazed in through the opening, it seemed especially strange that there were no lights of any kind on, in, or around the Cromwell house. He studied the open yard looking for the best way to approach the house with the least chance of being spotted. He determined that they should follow the fence line along the side of the yard to his left which had a slight shadow and would lead him directly to the detached garage and ultimately to safe cover.

Stooping over and staying fairly low as they hastily made their break along the fence, they reached the back corner of the garage in less than a minute. Austin stood at the left rear corner. Yi Fun was directly behind him. Austin took a peek toward the back of the house.

"I don't see any activity out here." Stephen's whispered voice came through the ear buds. "It doesn't look like you were noticed."

Austin took another peek at the house and determined that the easiest access point to the house was the door on the side between the garage and the house.

He also knew that it would be armed with an alarm. Unfortunately the best option, best being defined by the point least likely to have a security clip on it, was a second floor window just above the back porch roof. He looked back at Yi Fun and pointed to the roof. She acknowledged, put her Ruger away then stepped in front of Austin and headed to the nearest support post.

To the right of the post was a small two-person wrought-iron bench which she picked up quickly and moved over close to the post. She immediately sprung up on the bench, swung around the post and kicked her legs high up into the air and pushed herself up to the edge of the roof ending up on her stomach. Austin was stunned. "Awesome!" said Stephen apparently watching their every movement and not realizing he'd said it out loud.

"I know, right?" replied Austin. "But, keep your eyes open for the bad guys, please."

Austin looked up at Yi Fun whose gloved hands were reaching down toward him. He moved the bench to the outside of the post and stepped up. He reached up to her outstretched arms and made a good strong hold then whispered, "On three." He nodded his head slightly once, then again, then with a large nod he leapt just as Yi Fun tugged providing just enough help to get Austin securely onto the roof's edge from the waist up. Yi Fun moved away allowing Austin to work his way further onto the roof.

They took a moment to catch their breath before taking a good long look at the window located at the top of the porch roof. Upon closer examination they determined there was no alarm patch but they also realized that it was a screened, dual pane window. The worst part was that it was built similar to a dormer and that it was locked. After a short, silent discussion, Yi Fun and Austin elected to make it open. They removed the screen from the window and placed it carefully and securely on the roof, making sure that it did not slide off. Then, taking out his pistol, Austin took the barrel in his right hand and put his left arm against the glass and slightly above where the rotating lock was located. He drew the weapon back to what he felt was the minimum required distance to break the glass then in an instant tapped the glass through his shirt sleeve.

Most of the glass fell away and into the room landing quietly on the carpet below. There were medium sized fragments lying around the pane and lock. Austin reached inside and unlocked the window then gently slid it upward until it had reached its peak. Yi Fun had taken her left glove off and handed it to Austin to brush away any remnants of glass before they proceeded. Austin then stuck his head in just enough to get a complete view of the entire room.

Comfortable that there was no one inside, Austin

stepped through the open window, left leg first, then right, being careful to avoid the scattered glass lying on the carpet beneath the window. Once inside he kept watch and assessed the room for hiding places while Yi Fun followed him through the window. Austin motioned Yi Fun to the closet located to her right while he backed away from the window along the edge of the bed and moved closer to the open doorway. He caught a glimpse of Yi Fun out of the corner of his eye as she opened the closet door then stepped away. The closet was completely full of clothes and boxes but otherwise of no importance. Yi Fun took a quick look under the bed which was also stuffed with boxes and clear storage containers.

"Everything still quiet out here," came Stephen's voice in their ear buds as Austin looked over at the night stand.

He waived Yi Fun over then whispered in her ear, "Strange. Power is clearly on." He pointed at the nightstand next to the bed and the digital alarm clock brightly displaying 11:51PM. "Not a light on in the house; not even a nightlight. They may be expecting us." He pulled the Glock 31, 357 automatic from his back. Yi Fun instantly pulled out the Ruger P89 thinking she'd keep the 45 for later in the game.

Stepping back to the doorway, Austin took a quick peek right then left, then pulled his head back inside. From the brief assessment he was able to determine that the upstairs had three bedrooms and at least one bath although he suspected that the larger room, located at the other end of the floor plan probably had a private bath. Austin motioned for Yi Fun to watch while he crossed the hall into the second bedroom. Once inside, Yi Fun followed while keeping a peripheral look to the hallway.

After clearing the second bedroom they moved back out into the hallway and began their calculated sweep of the rest of the floor. Yi Fun moved down the hallway with her back against the left side wall while Austin was stooped a bit and against the right side. With their eyes adjusting to the darkness inside the house they could see that the bathroom door to the right was located directly across from the stairwell which led to the first floor below. Austin had the better angle on the bathroom door while Yi Fun could keep watch on the stairs.

Making their way to the hallway edge of the stairs, Austin took a careful look inside the small bathroom and could not see anyone inside. He looked at Yi Fun who motioned to him that the stairs seemed clear as well. Austin turned to face the bath with his back firmly against the wall and sent a silent signal for Yi Fun to enter the bath which she immediately did. Moments later she stepped out the doorway and they instantly moved pass the bath and down the hallway to the open doorway to the last bedroom.

Yi Fun provided support as Austin leapt inside first. Yi Fun quickly followed. The bed was still made. Austin quickly checked the master bath while Yi Fun investigated the walk-in closet. No sign of Cromwell anywhere on this floor. Austin tugged on Yi Fun's arm then led her to the double sink in the master bathroom. He pointed at the empty tooth brush holders. There was no shaving cream or razor, no antiperspirant, no hair brushes or makeup kits or blow-driers.

Feeling more like they'd been setup, they moved their attentions to the first floor. Descending the stairs, careful not to hit a set dead center as that was the most likely place to cause a creaking noise, they made the turn at the landing halfway down. The stairway opened into a large, well decorated great-room with a fire-place located in a corner at the back of the room and to the left. To the right was an open kitchen and Austin could see beyond that was a utility room with at least a washer and he assumed a dryer.

There was a small hallway to the right of the stairs that led back toward the front of the house and Austin could see a doorway to what he thought might be the dining room. As he stood near the bottom of the stairs there was a wall to his left that beyond was clearly an-other room. He elected to check it last as the great room, kitchen and utility room were the quickest rooms to eliminate as hiding places.

Once the utility room was cleared by Austin he turned toward the dining room which Yi Fun had already secured. She motioned him through the dining room and pointed to the other door leading out toward the stairs. From his vantage point Austin could clearly see the front door and part of the porch through the sheer curtains on the window. Yi Fun again motioned for Austin to move on around. Austin moved to within inches of Yi Fun's right shoulder, her arms outstretched with both hands holding the Ruger fairly low but readied.

Yi Fun rolled around Austin allowing him to slide forward to the inner edge of the second doorway. With his Glock lowered toward the floor he narrowed his body, moved his forehead right up to the edge of the door facing, then glanced around the framing and into the foyer. Across the foyer about eight feet was a closed door to the final room. To the right was the hallway leading back to the great room and Austin could see that there was apparently another half bath built under the stairs. *Too small to for anyone to hide in with the door open like that,* he thought and ignored it.

They slowly inched their way over to the seemingly menacing door. Yi Fun stood to the left of the door and against the outside wall almost directly in front of a window, straining to keep from moving the curtains.

Austin stepped to the right, put his weapon in his left hand and the door knob in his right. Yi Fun and Austin again made eye contact. He nodded once, then again, then on the third nod he turned the knob and pushed the door open just a bit, just enough for Yi Fun to see part of the room and position herself.

Yi Fun stooped low to the floor, gun raised and pointed toward the door. Austin stepped closer to her and moved into the doorway, put his pistol back into his right hand, then slowly pushed the door open wider revealing more of the room. Austin darted in through the door and into the room with Yi Fun shadowing and to Austin's right.

They'd made almost no discernable sound at all as they made their way through the house and ultimately into this room which turned out to be an office with a large desk and two chairs directly in front. It was the chair behind the desk that had Austin's attention. The figure sitting at the desk, completely unaware of their presence, was stooped to his left, a pin light stuck in his mouth and his head apparently looking into the bottom drawer of the executive desk. Finally as Austin and Yi Fun moved closer to the desk the figure looked up and directly at Austin. The dark figure froze in place. Yi Fun's Luger swept up and came to a stop with the barrel pointing directly at the silhouette. Austin's chin dropped. "Nick?"

CHAPTER TWENTY

Tuesday, June 16th, 5:30 p.m. thru 12:30 a.m.
Wednesday, June 17th

Except for the delivery of the listening equipment provided by Director Hughes, the evening had been pretty quiet. So uneventful in fact that each of the agents took turns catching some shut eye, while the others watched and listened for anything unusual. The listening equipment consisted of a directional antenna with a small receiving dish and both linked to a receiver-booster combination. The specialized head phones plugged into the booster as well, enabling the wearer to hear anything from specific transmitting frequencies while blocking out all other sound.

Blackwell, after verbalizing his wish that they'd been supplied with 'eyes' too, accepted the gifts they'd been given and chose to take the first shift to listen. He had the antenna pointed directly at the home currently occupied by the Moroccans. There was so little activity that occasionally Harris would have to give him a nudge to keep him awake. There were a few brief moments when a 'ting' or 'thump' would break the otherwise noiseless void, but each time there came nothing to follow. Thinking it wise, he occasionally would sweep the antenna around toward the Cromwell home in the event someone decided to pay the now abandoned home a private visit but the results were always the same, negative.

The Hidden Valley entrance was just as boring to Harris. He'd carefully watched through his binoculars each of the vehicles that left the development and several that entered and not one carried any of the men they'd seen at the warehouse. While he considered himself a patient man, the stench from his sweat-laden clothing combined with his lack of sleep were beginning to take a toll and his perception of the complete lack of progress they've made on this case was beginning to magnify his frustration.

The Prius was still home to Rachael as she had chosen to stay in the front seat and recline in order to get some sleep. This, she said would free up plenty of space in the back seat of the Ford to set up the sound equipment. It had worked out well for her since, of the three, she seemed to be the one who had gotten the most rest. As she slowly woke from her less than comfortable slumber, neck stiff, mouth dry and hair stuck to the side of her face, she looked over at Harris and Blackwell still hard at work, *staying awake,* she thought.

She raised the backrest of the front seat and shifted herself around, pulled down the visor with the lighted-mirror and freshened up her look. The guys hadn't even seemed to notice that she had awakened. *Doesn't matter; got work to do myself before I let one of the guys take a break,* she thought to herself. She reached over into the passenger seat and picked up her phone, still plugged into the car charger from when she first drove off with the rented automobile. She pressed the button on the side to light up the screen so that she could read the clock. It was 8:38 p.m.

She realized that Greg was already gone for the night but thought she'd give his desk a call, maybe she'd get lucky and someone would answer and be able to give her an update. Before she could unplug the phone from the charger the phone began to ring.

"Agent Birch," she answered.

"Hey, Rachael. This is Director Hughes." He hesitated for just a second then continued. "Have you still got eyes on the Armenians?"

"Yes sir. Agent Harris is keeping eyes on the entrances for both Shady Acres and Hidden Valley. Agent Blackwell is monitoring using the equipment you sent. Thanks for that, by the way."

"Well, you may also find it helpful to know that the day we extracted Cromwell we also sent a crew to his home. We had them place several transmitters around the place. Anyone goes in I think you should be able to pick it up on the monitor, especially if they get within six to eight feet of them."

"That's good to know, sir. Blackwell has mostly been focusing on the Armenians but we'll try to sweep both." Rachael started to ask if there was anything else as she was in a hurry to update the guys and she was ready for a potty break but the director was not ready to let her go.

"Ok. Now to the important news. We finally got the Cole file opened. Well, as opened as we were going to get it," he said, qualifying his statement. "Mr. Cole is not what he seems. We do know that he was at some point CIA. However, at some point he either went deep cover or to some other agency. Either way, they won't open that part of the file."

"So, at the very least he's CIA?" asked Rachael, not really sure what all that meant to her case.

"We don't think he's active now. He apparently was deactivated some three years ago but again, the agency he was working with at the time of his departure still has his entire file classified."

"So what would a former agent turned cowboy be doing mixed up with these arms dealers?" Rachael asked, while even more questions were popping into her head. "Do you think he's still active and undercover?"

"We just don't know," responded the Director. "There's no evidence to support that. What we do know is that his house was broken into last Friday. We do know there is evidence that his young stepbrother is missing and we do know that for some reason he tried to pay Mr. Cromwell a visit twice: once at the college and once at his residence."

"We also know that his stepbrother apparently called Mr. Cromwell," Rachael added. "So he could be legitimately looking for his missing brother or he could be undercover or he could be working with the Armenians and somehow there's an MSS agent tied up in this as well." Rachael had summed it up pretty well and had only one more question to ask. "So, what do we do now?"

"You three stay put overnight. I'll have a few more teams on the ground by 10:00 a.m. your time tomorrow to give you a break. By this time tomorrow night there will be a squad there to take down the Armenians and we'll start getting some answers."

"Very well, sir. Thanks." Rachael hung up the phone.

Blackwell had moved to the Prius to try to get some sleep. Rachael had moved to the front seat with Harris who was still behind the wheel. It was now pretty late and there was very little traffic in the area. Most of the homes had turned most of the lights inside off, a clear indication that people were going to bed to get a good night of sleep. It was something Rachael was looking forward to, in less than twelve hours, she hoped.

With the new information about Cole fresh in her

mind and the knowledge that there had been transmitters placed inside the Cromwell home by an NSA
team, Rachael started splitting time pointing the directional antenna toward each of the target homes.
With no transmitters in the home occupied by the
Armenians she really didn't expect much from that
area and found herself spending more time with her
ears to Cromwell's.

By 11:30 p.m. she'd all but abandoned Hidden
Valley, Harris had dosed off and Blackwell was sound
asleep in the Prius. Rachael had managed to stay awake
but she was foggy and was it not for the occasional
sound in her ear to prop her eyelids open she too
would be blissfully napping. It was at just one of those
moments when a short series of tingling sounds similar to loose change dropping to the floor came blaring
through her headphones. He eyes widened immediately. Without realizing it she seemed to straighten up in
her seat. All of her senses were suddenly heightened.

She carefully listened for further confirmation. She
waited. There. There it is. Then back to silence. She
knew she didn't imagine it but she also didn't know
if it was anything more than just a mouse knocking
something over, either way, until she knew more she
wasn't going to wake the guys. She continued to focus,
listening as closely as she could for any sound that she
could recognize and identify. There it was. The clear

sound of a squeak, the kind that a creaking floor panel makes when one of the boards are loose and someone just stepped onto it then off again.

"Harris," she said as she pushed him slightly on his shoulder. "Harris. Wake up."

He waited for his eyes to catch up then turned to Rachael. "What's wrong?"

Rachael responded immediately, handing the headphones to Harris. "I think someone's in the Cromwell house."

Harris slid the headphones over his ears and waited patiently for something that would confirm Agent Birch's conclusion. A long quiet moment went by, then another, and another. Then his eyebrows raised and his eyes widened. "Let's check it out," he said even as he was taking the headphones off. "Get Blackwell."

Agent Birch opened her door, slid out of her seat and stepped over to the Prius just close enough to start tapping on the window. Agent Blackwell was a bit slower to react than Harris but realized immediately that something was up. He raised the seat, opened the door then darted into the back seat of the Ford just as Rachael was strapping into the front.

"We're going to pull into Shady Acres, park the car near the bridge just beyond Cromwell's street," said Harris already crossing into traffic. "Next, we're going to hoof it up to the house." Nobody said anything. Just as they pulled into Shady Acres Estates the car started to slow and Harris began to issue more instructions. "When we get to the house, Tim, you take the back door, I'll take the front, and Rachael, you take the side entrance coming in from the garage." Everyone nodded that they understood and all three agents got out of the vehicle and started the long walk illuminated only by the quarter moon above and an occasional street light.

Once the agents got close to the residence they made their way to the garage. Offset from the home and back a bit further from the road, it provided a good bit more cover both by shade and location relative to the home. Blackwell went around to the right and came up on the back side of the garage making sure that he maintained contact with the rear of the building itself so that he could stay in the shadows. Agent Birch was close behind with the intent of trailing off when the corner gave way to the open breezeway between the garage and the side entrance to the home.

Harris had the shortest route to take but it was also the most dangerous as there was little cover between the front of the garage and the door at the front of the house. The degree of difficulty increased as a result of the many tall windows which lined the front of the home and no lights on inside. Because there was a front porch on the dwelling and set above ground level by about two feet, he was able to stoop low and brush along the shrubbery lining the front and either side of the stairs. As soon as he found an opening large enough to get onto the porch and into the shadow it provided, Harris had every intention of taking it. Unfortunately, the closest opportunity was located dead center of the length of the porch at the stairs, directly in front of the door.

Staying as low to the ground as he could, Agent Harris slid stomach down onto the porch floor and then up next to the door where he stood next to the door frame. He composed himself, readied his weapon and listened for activity inside to try to get a feel for where the intruders may be. All was quiet. He could hear the hedge brushing against the floor panels of the front porch with each slight breeze but then nothing. He decided to give Agents Birch and Blackwell time to get into place before he went in.

Birch was in place well before Harris and Blackwell as once she turned the back corner nearest the house she simply took four quick steps to the stairs at the side entrance and waited. She was to wait until she heard one of the other agents call out then she was to enter from the side. She was nervous even though her weapon was steady and her breathing controlled. She'd never had to use her weapon in the field before but, *I guess the training's paying off,* she thought. She sneaked a quick look in through the small window in the upper third area of the door but saw nothing of any use.

She evaluated the door and determined that when it was time she'd have to open the storm door from left to right then kick in the inner door, again something she'd never had to do before.

From the back of the garage to the rear entrance to the house was only about twenty feet. There was an overhang for a small porch roof over a small patio area and almost all of the area was under cover of shadow so he was able to move fairly quickly. His area of concern was a pair of standard windows between him and the door. One of the two windows was really a half window which he guessed was located above the sink in the kitchen or in the utility room and the other was probably at the breakfast area near the kitchen. It was a taller window with a lower base than the other and he knew he'd have to maneuver around it carefully to insure that he was not seen. Moments later the three agents were in place.

CHAPTER TWENTY ONE

Wednesday June 17th, 1:08 a.m.

Nick exploded out of his seat upon hearing Austin's voice. His right index finger sprung to his lips. His eyes widened, keeping his finger in place he turned his head and pointed with his left hand in an arc then shook his head. He pointed at his ears then again pointed around the room. He looked Austin directly in the eyes then motioned for him to move closer. Yi Fun stayed in place, her gun still in position, her eyes and ears still wide open and perked. As Austin moved toward his brother, taking care not to make a sound, he heard a crackle in his ear-bud and suddenly froze.

"Guys, thought you might find it interesting that I just spotted a guy in a second floor window of a house in the subdivision next to this one and he seems really curious about the Cromwell house." Stephen reached in his bag and pulled out a larger, more powerful scope, lowered his rifle just enough to get the new scope to his eyes. "He looks foreign. He's using some really expensive binoculars and from what I can see in the room there appears to be weapons staged against a wall. Figured you should know. Everything else seems quiet." The ear-bud fell silent.

Austin looked over at Yi Fun with a look of acknowledgement then turned his attention back to Nick. "It doesn't matter if they hear us. They already know we're here. What are you doing here?"

"I came looking for Cromwell. Got here Sunday but had to lay low because some goons came looking for him, too," replied Nick, his eyes still darting left then right. "Look, we've got to get out of here. And we need to do it fast."

Yi Fun stepped forward slightly. "We have company."

Austin turned his head back over his shoulder toward Yi Fun but never took his eyes off Nick. "Yeah. I know. Three of them. You take the one at the front door. I'll take the back and the side." He turned to face Nick and said in his most serious tone, "You get under that desk and stay there, no matter what happens, until I come back and get you." Nick nodded and moved quickly back behind the desk and watched as Austin turned and walked over to Yi Fun. "If you can help it, let's try not to hurt anyone," said Austin as he moved toward the door which lead from the office into the great room and disappeared into the shadows.

Yi Fun inched her way over to the front door which was located just to her right and outside the office door near the front wall. She realized that the front door would open directly toward her so she'd need to get to the other side of the door frame to be in the best position to address her attacker. She decided to stoop low to the floor and move back down the hallway next to the bath so as to stay in the shadows created by the stairs. Once past them she positioned herself at the front wall between the window and the front door and waited for her assailant to make their move.

Austin chose to go straight to the back door off the great room as it was closest to the office and therefore closest to Nick. He'd deal with the utility room access when he had to. Staying low behind the sofa, he followed its lines to the landing at the door way to the porch. He could plainly see the silhouette of a man holding a gun just outside the mostly glass, French-style doors. He stood to the left of the fixed door realizing that only one would open.

An instant later the door swung open abruptly, smashing against the wall next to the kitchen and Agent Blackwell leapt inside. Austin immediately dislodged the firearm from Blackwell's hand, took hold of his arm with his right hand then quickly spun counterclockwise into him to deliver an elbow bluntly against the left temple of Blackwell's head. The elbow was followed quickly by a leg sweep taking Agent Blackwell to the floor, already nearing unconsciousness. With Austin still in control of his right arm, he stepped across his prostrate body and while twisting his arm at the wrist quickly kicked him across the side of the head to finish the job.

Hearing the back door being kicked in, Yi Fun prepared herself and seconds later the front door, too, burst open. As Agent Harris sprung into the foyer Yi Fun grabbed his gun-yielding wrist and immediately smashed his forearm with her elbow. While still holding him she stabbed his midsection with her right knee and as he bent forward and out of breath she quickly delivered the bottom of the handle of her Ruger P89 to the back of Agent Harris's head. In seconds he was unconscious, lying flat on his stomach on the floor and Yi Fun was heading to the great room to help Austin.

Yi Fun quickly rounded the corner and ran down the short hallway to the kitchen, looked first left to the great room where there seemed to be no activity and then to the right toward the utility room and where Austin said the third uninvited guest would be. The kitchen was about fifteen feet from the great room end to the opening to the utility room. Even in the dark, she could see all the way through the kitchen, through the utility room and outside to the wall of the garage.

She slowly walked into the kitchen, gun drawn, eyes open wide, barely able to see the dark figure standing, no, leaning against the refrigerator near the open door. As she got closer she could see Austin with his left arm wrapped across his chest and lightly grasping his right arm, still holding his Glock but in a somewhat casual manner. Yi Fun could see that he was strangely looking toward the center of the floor just beyond the island bar located in the center of kitchen with chairs located on one side which obstructed her view from whatever Austin was looking at.

As she made her approach, not a word was being spoken. In fact, there was no discernable sound at all. She stepped past the first of the chairs and then could see, sitting on the floor, knees slightly bent and leaning up on her elbows was a young woman who clearly seemed to be contemplating trying to reach the standard issue firearm lying on the floor not three feet from where she'd fallen. "I would not recommend that," said Yi Fun as she stepped around Agent Birch and over to Austin.

"You ok?" asked Austin as Yi Fun leaned against the counter next to him.

"Sure. No one seriously hurt. Maybe a headache later." Yi Fun replied.

There was a short pause in conversation and no reaction at all from the agent sitting below them. "The other two are NSA agents. I recognize them from their visit to my home just after Nick disappeared." He paused, seemed liked he was biting the inside of his lip, squinted his eyes and said, "But this one, I don't know who she is."

"Perhaps we should ask?" offered Yi Fun.

"Good idea but we haven't got much time for a conversation." Austin stepped forward and knelt beside the unarmed agent confident that Yi Fun could keep him covered. "So who are you and why are you after me?"

Agent Birch looked at Austin, then beyond him to Yi Fun. "I'm not really sure who you are, but we've been looking for her. She's a Chinese MSS Agent." She didn't move but looked Austin directly in the eyes. "I know that your name is Austin Cole and that there is some kind of locked agency file on you that even we can't get authorities to open." She looked back to Yi Fun. "And we can't help but wonder what a Chinese spy who's in this country illegally and a purported construction manager from Brookeland, Texas, with a sealed security file is doing in the same home as a retired NASA manager. Makes us wonder if maybe you're working together on something we wouldn't like."

Austin studied her for a few seconds then stood straight up. "We haven't got time for this," he said, as he lowered the gun in his right hand and offered Agent Birch his left and pulled her to her feet. "Look, we've got to get out of here right now. You can't stop us and you need to know what we've got to tell you." Austin instructed Yi Fun to go get Nick. Austin moved over to

Agents Birch's left, bent down and picked up her gun then stuck it firmly in the waistline of his pants just as Nick and Yi Fun entered the room. "You can go with us or stay here."

Agent Birch watched as Nick and Yi Fun walked passed her. "I really don't have much of a choice, do I?" she asked, looking down at her gun resting firmly under Austin's shirt.

"You'll get your gun back and your phone as soon as we reach our car."

Rachael hadn't even noticed that he'd taken her phone out of her pocket. She quickly checked to make sure. The pocket was empty.

Austin watched. "It's your choice." Rachael hesitated a moment then followed Yi Fun out the side door through the utility room with Austin tagging close behind.

"I see you have some new friends," said Stephen watching them exit the home and move back through the yard toward the point they initially entered.

Austin touched his microphone. "Don't watch us. Watch the house and the other house. I think we'll be seeing them fairly soon." Overhearing Austin even though he was almost whispering, Agent Birch glanced back as if she had a thousand questions but elected to keep walking. A short ten minute hike along the canal and back under the bridge then up to the Challenger, still hidden in the shadows behind the women's clinic, and the journey was over.

"Now what?" asked Agent Birch. She walked over to the car and leaned against the fender.

Austin turned to Nick. "Right now, I need to know what you were thinking!" Austin had come almost nose-to-nose with Nick. "Do you have any idea what we've been through trying to find you?" Clearly a rhetorical question and one Nick recognized as best being left unanswered. "It doesn't matter." Austin shook his head slightly as if trying to calm down. "Look, you are going to stay here with Agent Birch," he said to Nick as he looked directly at Rachael, "and she's going to keep you safe until we get back. Do you understand?"

Nick nodded but immediately responded. "Listen, it's dangerous out there. I think there are some really bad guys watching that Cromwell house."

"How would you know that?" asked Austin.

"I've been here, off and on, since Saturday. I've never seen Cromwell. I even went to the college to try to talk with him but couldn't get in." Nick changed his tone slightly. "The only people I've seen come to his house are some cable guys, which in hind sight I don't think were cable guys, and these rough looking men."

"What did they do?" Austin again glanced at Yi Fun.

"Two just sat in the SUV while the other two went to the door and knocked but nobody answered. They always came in the early evening, though, like they knew when he should be getting home from school."

"Do you know what they're looking for?" asked Agent Birch trying to get something solid out of the conversation that she didn't already know.

Austin immediately stepped in before Nick could answer, took him by the arm and pulled him to one side. "Nick, I want you to stay with Agent Birch," he said, just loud enough that he knew Birch could hear, "and tell her everything you know." Then his voice lowered just below her ability to hear. "Don't tell her anything about EMPTEC. That may be our only way out of this." He turned Nick back around and walked him over to Agent Birch.

"Ok, you can believe this or not but here's our story. I've just spent the last four days looking for my brother," he pointed at Nick. "We've found him. Now, Yi Fun and I are going to go find her brother which we believe is being held by some arms dealers in a house in the subdivision just beyond Mr. Cromwell's." He looked at Nick then reached into his front pocket and turned back to Agent Birch. "Here is your cell phone. Your partners should be waking up pretty soon. They'll be trying to reach you. I need you to watch after Nick. Keep him safe."

"What are you going to do?" asked Agent Birch, knowing the answer but asking anyway.

"Yi Fun and I are going to go get her brother. I need to know that you are going to protect Nick. He's going to tell you everything he knows. Just keep him safe." Austin reached under his shirt and pulled the NSA agent's weapon from his waist and handed it to her, grip first.

"Listen, it's the fourth house on the right. It's a two story home with a basement garage. The driveway is to the left." Agent Birch felt strangely compelled to give Austin all the details she had. "There were at least two black SUVs parked there when I drove through. We know that there are at least four men inside but our best guess is seven." Austin started to turn away. "Mr. Cole, we're pretty sure that they are heavily armed and well trained mercenaries so be very careful."

"Give us ten minutes to get there," Austin spoke calmly, "another thirty to neutralize the targets, and another ten to get back."

"And if I haven't heard from you in an hour?"

Briefly glancing back over his shoulder to Agent Birch, "Send in everybody," Austin calmly replied, then climbed over the fence and down into the canal.

CHAPTER TWENTY TWO

Wednesday June 17th, 2:28 a.m.

"Stephen, you still in place?" asked Austin.

"Yep," replied Stephen. "Nothing's changed. Ugly man in the window with binoculars. No other activity around either house."

"Good. Keep your eyes open. We're heading back in and going to try to make it to the other house. Let us know if you see something. Otherwise we're going silent."

Austin and Yi Fun had just passed under Shady Acres Circle. The shadows in the canal had changed a bit over the hour and a half since they'd initially made the walk. The small, tilted concrete walls of the narrow canal were now easily visible making their trek from one end of Shady Acres to the other far more danger-ous. Austin did feel confident that even with high pow-ered binoculars the 'man in the window' would not be able to see into the canal until they were almost to the other side of the subdivision.

They chose to walk as close to the left side of the canal wall as possible as it provided the worst line-of-sight from the target house and therefore their best defense against being seen. The ten minute trek took them about fifteen but they reached the opposite bridge and were standing under it at the opening on the Hidden Valley side. Getting out of the canal on the Hidden Valley side was beginning to look a bit more difficult as there were concrete walls at both ends that extended up to and level with the privacy fencing for the adjacent properties. Austin was beginning to think they'd have to walk further down the canal to find a way in but Yi Fun had another idea.

"At this opening between the two bridges," she said, pointing midway back under the bridge, "there is a privacy fence that separates the two subdivisions. I saw that there is a large tree planted on this side of that fence that has a long limb drooping down. With your help I may be able to reach it."

Austin smiled, immediately realizing what she was thinking. "Let's do it," he said, having already started back under the bridge.

Standing in the center of the opening between the two bridges, Austin could clearly see the long tree limb hanging down over the section of privacy fence connecting the two bridges. He was not sure it would be long enough even if they were able to get to it, but it was worth a try. Yi Fun stood next to the canal wall. Austin placed one foot forward and bent his knee, then interlocking his fingers, placed both hands palms up, onto his knee.

Yi Fun placed her left hand on Austin's right shoulder then put her left foot into his waiting hands. She looked once again at the tree limb and then to Austin, who said, "On three. One, two, three." Yi Fun sprang upward as Austin provided the extra lift she needed and seconds later she was descending with both hands holding tightly to the curving limb.

As soon as she was in arms' reach Austin began pulling Yi Fun down, first pulling her legs then her hips, then a shoulder and finally, able to grasp the tree with one hand, he pulled the limb as hard as he could. Yi Fun's feet came to rest on the canal floor just after Austin had secured the limb with both hands and leaned back as far as he could. Yi Fun didn't wait for Austin. She started pulling herself up the side of the canal wall, then up the wooden fence and stooped at the top holding the limb and roosting on one of the fence posts.

Austin followed with a bit more difficulty than Yi Fun, but just as he was reaching the top of the fence, Yi Fun jumped to the ground on the other side. Austin jumped after her coming to rest near the trunk of the tree and behind some large hedges trimmed to look like large spheres. They stooped low for cover, still under the shadow of the huge tree, and evaluated their surroundings.

They started back down the fence line, staying in

the shadows naturally provided by the large trees until they came to the first fenced lot. The road had curved away from them creating the spacing to put a home on this side of the street. The house just past this one was their target but they were not sure how they were going to get to it unnoticed. They couldn't go through the fence before them and there was no side walk on this side of the street. If they crossed to the other side, they would be in plain view of their prey. The only other choice they had was to walk as quickly and quietly along the front of the first home to get to the target.

Austin led the way, staying low and feeling a slight bit of relief upon seeing the matching wood fencing on the other side of the home delineating the lot lines between the two homes. The corner of the fence protected them from view from both houses. *With any luck nobody on that side sees us,* Austin thought, taking a brief pause and looking across the street.

A quick glance around the corner of the fence netted Austin a snapshot of what they were going to face. As Agent Birch had told them, there was a front porch which ran the length of the house at ground level. There was also a basement garage off the driveway to the left of the home but the garage doors had been replaced using brick which matched the rest of the basement. Between what used to be the garage door openings was a standard access door and a porch light located directly above and to the right of the door. He could also see two dark colored SUVs in the driveway, one of which he recognized from his short ride earlier the day before. That SUV was parked down close to the side basement entrance. The other was parked at the apex of the driveway up near the street.

A good forty feet of open yard lay between Austin and the basement door and perhaps thirty to the front door. The only cover they'd have would be the two SUVs and they wouldn't have that until they were almost at the doors. Yi Fun tapped Austin's shoulder and pointed at the SUV near the street.

"If one of us could make it there we would have a better view from which to plan our attack," said Yi Fun, almost sitting on the ground behind the kneeling Austin.

"I'll go. Wait here for my signal." Austin darted to the right rear quarter panel of the SUV then moved around the rear to the other corner. He couldn't see any lights on in the house and there was no evidence of a guard keeping watch on the front. The four front windows on the lower floor were well covered and Austin saw no gaps in the curtains. *That means they're probably not even looking for someone from the front,* thought Austin, who had already started looking to the second floor above the porch roof.

There were two dormers on the second floor, both

with curtains and no discernable light. He decided that the dormers were purely for show and nonfunctional but decided it was worth the risk to check in with Stephen. He depressed the pin on his shirt which activated the microphone. "Stephen, how many windows on the second floor?"

His answer was short and direct. "Two single bedroom windows and one smaller in between them that I suspect is a bathroom."

"What about the first floor and the basement?"

"There is a large deck coming off the center of the house on the first floor. Two large windows to the right of the deck. That is, the right as I'm looking at it."

Austin smiled. "What about to the left side?"

"Those three look like they may be kitchen or dining room windows," Stephen responded. "They look a bit shorter." Stephen tilted his scope a down a bit. "There looks to be two windows in the basement, one on either side of the deck. I would bet the stairs are located in between them, too."

"Any lights on that you can see?"

"Nope. Although the basement windows don't seem to have any curtains on them. And the first floor windows have blinds that look half shut." Stephen paused. "Hmm, French-style doors must be a big thing here."

Again, Austin smiled. He turned back to the other side of the SUV and motioned Yi Fun to join him. In a flash she was kneeling beside him at the back of the vehicle. He traded places with her so that she could get as good a look. He knew she'd heard the conversation he'd just had with Stephen so she was aware of the layout.

"My guess is there are five or six guys in there. I think there are two bedrooms upstairs, a master bedroom on the first floor. So, three or four are probably sleeping. We know one is in the first bedroom keeping an eye on Cromwell's. That leaves one or two sleeping in the living room or standing guard." Austin took off his backpack, opened up several of the compartments and began pulling out extra clips and his other hand gun. Yi Fun began doing the same thing. Austin touched the microphone pin. "Stephen. You there?"

One brief crackle later came, "Yep. You guys there yet?"

"We're getting ready to go in." Austin looked over at Yi Fun who never made eye contact. "You pack up and head back to the car with Nick. I left him with an NSA Agent. The two from inside the house are probably there or will be shortly. You need to get there before they leave with Nick."

"On it." Stephen pulled off the headphones, started packing and was on his way in three minutes.

After placing the extra clips in his socks and at various spots between his belt loops he ditched the bag and looked to the house. "Before we go in, I'm going to check that basement door to see if it's accessible. You follow me but keep going to the back of the house. Look for a quiet way in. I'll either go in through the side door or the front." Austin glanced again around the corner toward the basement. "One more thing. I know this is about to get ugly but let's try not to kill anyone."

Yi Fun's expression was self-explanatory. She nodded anyway and placed her 45 in the back of her waist band, picked up her Luger, took the safety off and leaned forward ready to advance. She turned toward Austin, waiting for his 'go' and said, "So which agency did you work for?"

Seemingly reluctant to answer he made sure there was a round in the chamber of his Glock 31. Then he targeted the door, took a deep breath and said, "All of them."

He darted around Yi Fun and toward the basement door. Yi Fun was close behind. Both followed the lines created by the two vehicles trying to blend in. Once they reached the front of the SUV near the basement door, Yi Fun peeled off and went on to the back corner of the house. Austin rushed to the door knob of the basement door. He carefully moved it to see if it was loose and noisy. It was not. He gently turned the knob but his didn't turn. He reached in his pocket and pulled out his pocket knife, opened the smaller, thinner of the two blades and slid it between the door jam and the lock. With the lock in the open position he lightly pulled on the door. It didn't move. He then pushed. Still no movement.

Convinced the door was sealed from the inside somehow, he resigned himself to the fact that his way in would have to be through the front. He could see that Yi Fun had been waiting to determine his success or failure. He nodded and she disappeared around the corner. Austin moved to the front corner of the porch. As he sat in the neatly landscaped flower bed which wrapped the corner of the porch, Austin started to lunge onto the porch when he saw on the ground in front of him a small, bluish ceramic rabbit about the size of a football. His decision was instantaneous.

The front window off to the left side of the porch suddenly exploded then came crashing down splattering all over the porch and onto the floor and furniture inside. Just then the two men who'd been sleeping in the room sprung to their feet, pulled their guns, looked at the broken window and then spotted the ceramic rabbit lying on the floor near their feet. At that very instant Austin had kicked in the front door, sprung inside and fired one round to his right hitting one silhouetted man in the knee bringing him instantly to the floor.

Just as he turned toward the other room, a bullet raced by him taking part of his shirt and leaving a burning sensation on his upper left deltoid. He quickly fired two shots one to each knee of one of the men in the other room. Seeing the stairway before him, Austin instinctively dove into the living room barely missing being shot in the head from the gunman at the top of the stairs. He quickly slid behind a recliner for cover and was instantly greeted by three bullets ripping through the back of the chair missing his face by mere inches. Suddenly the gunfire ended and there was a sudden 'thud'. Austin snapped around the edge of the recliner, Glock readied but the only standing target was Yi Fun. At her feet was one man unconscious and another wreathing in pain from the two bullets he'd received from Austin.

By now the only sounds that could be heard were the screams of pain coming from the two injured mercenaries. Yi Fun signaled Austin that she'd take the basement while Austin decided to take the stairs to the second floor. He secured the weapons from the two gunmen in the living room, throwing them out the same broken window he'd thrown the rabbit through moments ago. He looked at the moaning man and kicked him in the head immediately quieting his moans.

Austin worked his way back toward the foyer to get the gun from the first victim but just before he could step through the door way he felt a punch to his forehead and he went flying backward tripping over a small table and falling to the floor. He knew in an instant who his attacker was but was unable to react fast enough to allude him. As his assailant pounced on him, throwing punch after punch, Austin recognized the familiar smell of cologne. He reached for a piece of the broken table and smashed it through 'Mr. Cologne Man's' left ear then threw him off to one side.

He quickly located his Glock, then surveyed the stairwell in case the men upstairs had started down. They hadn't so he turned back to his blood stained attacker, reaching down to check to see if his heart was still beating. Austin searched for the man's weapon but couldn't find it. He slid himself over to the wall near the stairwell.

Knowing he didn't want to make an easy target out of himself, he started looking for a diversion. As if reading his mind, Yi Fun had opened the door and made her way down the tiered stairs to the basement below. Just as she got near the last step the bullets started flying. Most bursting through the sheetrock walls, barely missing her by centimeters. The last bullet split the wall stud sending a mist of splinters into Yi Fun's left eye before she could cover her face.

Unable to see clearly out of her left eye she quickly tore a hole in the bottom of her shirt using the barrel site on her gun, then ripped off a long piece of the shirt. She wrapped the piece of clothing around her head and over her injured eye and tied it tightly then reached down for her weapon.

Her attacker was clearly shooting high, aiming for her head judging from the spray of bullets. She knelt as low as she could get while still maintaining her balance. Her head darted quickly from behind the wall then back but just long enough to make out her target's location. She carefully visualized her shot, took a deep breath then exhaled, darted from the stairs, rolled across the floor and fired one shot before seeking cover behind an old clothes washer. She could make out a weak, painful moan and then a loud call from nearby.

"Don't shoot. I'm unarmed." He repeated it just to be sure. "I'm unarmed. You shot the guy with the gun."

"Kick his weapon over to me then turn on a light so that I can see you," Yi Fin instructed, never leaving her position behind the washer. She could hear some rustling in the background then the skidding of the gun as it crossed the concrete floor toward the stairwell. A moment later the fluorescent lights began to flicker on. Yi Fun moved to the opposite side of the washer and took a quick glance around the corner then back.

Just as the gunfire erupted in the basement, Austin reached for a nearby magazine rack then quickly tossed it up the stairs. The moment the rack hit the stairs three quick rounds were fired down the stairs. As the third passed by Austin dove into the foyer and fired three rounds himself hitting the man at the top of the stairs in the upper right chest and once in the lower abdomen. He dropped immediately to the floor lying with his upper torso partially hanging down the stairs. *He'll bleed out if he stays like that,* Austin thought, then shook it off. He realized he had to get to the top of the stairs.

Austin leapt out the front door, put his Glock 31 in the small of his back, stepped up on the porch railing, and climbed the post to get to the roof. Once at the top of the porch he worked his way up to the dormer located toward the left end of the home. He took the long barrel end of his gun and broke out the window then quickly darted inside, rolled onto his shoulder and ended up on one knee with the gun held firmly with both hands and pointed directly at the entrance to the dormer hall.

He slowly moved toward the opening into the bedroom, inching his way near the corner, never taking his eyes off the entrance. The dormer hall was so narrow that he could not get an angle good enough to verify if there was anyone standing outside, in the bedroom, or near the doorway entering the bedroom. He looked around the hall for anything that he might use to his advantage. He saw a left over two-by-four and what looked to be an old, stained tee shirt. He wrapped the tee shirt around the end of the two-by-four then moved toward the entrance.

With his left hand firmly holding on to the end of the makeshift flag pole he quickly stuck the tee-shirt end through the opening then back. There was no response. He waited for a moment then tried again but this time at a point much higher off the floor. Suddenly there was a single 'popping' sound from a pistol followed by the jarring sensation of the bullet hitting the two-by-four. Austin dropped it immediately, stuck the barrel of his own gun around the corner near the very base of the door and fired three shots.

As he fired the last shot he dove out of the dormer hall and across the bedroom just barely being missed by the next two rounds fired into the bedroom from down the hallway. Austin couldn't tell if the gunman was in the bathroom or in the bedroom at the other end of the hall. He started to formulate a plan and kicked the footboard off the end of one of the twin beds. He picked it up to use it as a shield and moved over to the doorway.

Just as he was about to storm down the hall, the hallway light at the top of the stairway flashed on. Austin froze. He could clearly see the light switch from his vantage point on the way just above the first step. For his target to have turned on the lights he would have to have darted out of the bathroom, flipped the switch then darted back into the bathroom. Or, he could have dived down the stairs. *But I would have heard that,* thought Austin. *Must be someone else downstairs and my guy is still here.*

He slowly moved further down the hallway when two shots rang out with both bullets firmly planting themselves in the center of the wooden footboard. But from those two shots Austin could tell his assailant was clearly still in the bedroom at the end of the hall. As he got closer to the doorway to the bathroom and unfortunately also closer to the stairway, he set himself to the right side of the hallway.

Austin figured he still had 11 shots left in the clip. He took aim through the bathroom door at the mirrored wall just inside and over the sink. Starting as far back into the bathroom as he could, he started firing round after round in an erratic pattern but moving closer to the front with each round, then stopped abruptly as the big man dove out of the bedroom and into the hallway. Suddenly a tree of a man lunged out of the bedroom and darted toward Austin and the bed board knocking them both over. Though he was on his knees the big man threw the bullet hole riddled board off Austin and started to punch him, then froze in place when he noticed the Glock in Austin's hand pointed right at his chest.

Samir moved slowly backward and rose to his feet maintaining his readied stance, hoping to lunge again as soon as an opportunity presented itself. Austin sluggishly worked his way back to his feet holding the Glock in his right hand while instinctively reaching across his stomach to provide pressure for the now bloodied wound on his right side near his waist. Apparently one of those many bullets Samir fired made its way through the footboard of the bed hitting Austin just above the belt line. The line of dripping blood running through his open fingers, over his wrist and down Austin's hip was acting like a doggie treat to a little puppy, enticing Samir to make another attempt to get to Austin.

Having almost managed to reach his feet, Austin placed a bracing hand against the wall for support but allowed the barrel of his weapon to drop ever so slightly. Seeing the apparent weakness, Samir once again pounced. He kicked the now broken footboard toward Austin who, momentarily startled, fell back slightly falling against the wall and knocking the gun from his hand. Samir lunged forward, his right fist tightly clinched, ready for the killing blow to Austin's head. Austin stood erect and quickly leveraged himself, then swiftly blocked Samir's punch with his left hand while hitting him with an abrupt, short jab in the throat. Seconds later his opponent was on his knees then teetered over onto his face, coming to rest in a pool of blood stained carpet.

Austin let himself fall weakly back against the hallway wall, knees bent, wrists resting on top of his knees and his head down. He looked over the two motionless adversaries down the stairs and standing at the bottom he saw Yi Fun, gun in hand and a sly grin spread across her face.

"So, did you plan that?" asked Yi Fun as she glanced at Austin's handiwork and worked her way up the stairs toward the seated and still bleeding Austin.

Austin let a slight grin creep into the grimaced look, closed his eyes and lowered his head as if to take a restful, introspective moment. "Did you find your brother?"

"Yes. He's waiting under the tree at the canal," she replied stepping ever closer to the top of the stairs. "So, are you ok?" she asked, looking at the blood on his shirt and pants. "Are you going to need help getting out of here?"

"No," he said. "I'm ok. But you and your brother need to get out of here quick. We've got about 10 minutes before this place is crawling with NSA."

Yi Fun stooped near the top step. "I do not know where to go. Were it just me," she explained, "I could escape easily enough. But I don't think my brother could do it."

"Can't you get him back to China?"

"If he returns to China he will probably be humiliated and shunned as he did not succeed. Upon my return, I will surely be arrested and imprisoned as my trip here was not state sanctioned."

Austin thought for a moment and couldn't help but agree. "Well, if you stay in this country, the NSA is never going to stop looking for you. If your brother goes back to school the NSA will never stop watching his every move hoping he'll lead them to you, meaning no chance at a normal life." He shook his head. "Hell, as long as whoever these guys were working for believes that any of us know where that EMPTEC thing is, they'll never stop looking for any of us."

"Not very many choices," said Yi Fun, beginning to look a bit beaten.

"I think I may have a couple of ideas but I'm pretty sure you're not going to like any of them." Austin lifted himself to his feet. "I think we need to get started."

CHAPTER TWENTY THREE

Wednesday, June 17th, 3:17 a.m.

The darkness filling the canal under the bridge over Shady Acres Circle gave way to a lighter shade of grey as Stephen began his tenuous climb out of the canal, over the galvanized, chain-link fence and back up the dimly lit back street to the Challenger. Nick was dejectedly sitting on the hood of the challenger, his feet bracing against the bumper, his head resting in his hands. Agents Blackwell and Harris had managed to join Agent Birch who was busy doing her best to nurse the wounds they'd each received during their earlier activities.

Nick was the first to see Stephen as he stepped away from the fence and through the overgrown grass and weeds onto the pavement. He leapt from the car and was taking one of the bags from Stephen not four long strides later. The agents came to attention, starting to reach for their recovered weapons. Rachael calmed them and stepped forward to meet Stephen as he approached the car on his way to the trunk.

"Are they ok?" asked Nick. "Are they on their way back?"

Stephen nodded and kept walking until he'd reached the trunk, opened it and tossed both bags inside and the two handguns he'd carried with him. "We need to get going, now." Stephen looked sternly at Agent Birch and tossed her the keys to the Challenger that Austin had left with him. "If you have any friends around, it would be really great if they could come too."

"Wait, what's happened? Mr. Daniels," Nick pressed, "why are we leaving them?"

"Get in Nick. Now." Mr. Daniels grasped his arm. "Nothing to worry about, but we don't have time to waste."

Agent Birch opened the door, pulled the seat back forward and encouraged Nick to climb into the back seat followed immediately by Stephen. Agent Blackwell was already in the backseat having climbed in from the passenger side and Agent Harris was in the front seat already in the process of closing the door. "Where to?" asked Agent Birch as she started the car and began to back out of the dark alleyway.

"To get Austin," replied Stephen. "You need to call the police and get them over there."

Agent Harris was already dialing his cell before Stephen had completed his sentence. Agent Birch wasted no time with stop signs or red lights as she revved the HEMI and sped her way to Hidden Valley

Circle. The tires screamed and the rear of the vehicle lost traction slightly as she made the sharp left into the entrance and on the circle. Stephen was sure she hadn't used the brakes even once until she reached the subject residence.

Harris bailed before the car came to a halt with Blackwell leaping out immediately behind him. Both agents already had their weapons drawn and were approaching the house as Agent Birch exited the Challenger. "Stay here," she said, giving a slight glance to the back seat. "Don't either of you get out of this car. We have no idea what's going to happen here."

As they approached the house from across the front yard they could see that the interior, while poorly decorated and definitely in shambles, was well lit. It seemed that all the lights had been turned on and the front exterior door was standing wide open. Harris checked to the left side of the porch and could see clearly through the broken window, through the great room and to the open door at the back. The other agents had similar views as they moved closer to the porch and ultimately to the doorway leading into the foyer.

The screams of several men became more clearly defined with each step toward the house and as Agent Harris stepped through the doorway into the home, he could see three men lying on the floor in the great room, discolored holes near the knees of both men and puddles of blood surrounding them on the floor. There was another man, clearly unconscious, also lying on his stomach in a pool of blood. Harris backed out of the doorway to the great room and back into the foyer as Agents Birch and Blackwell followed inside. Blackwell went to the right into the dining room and followed a stream of blood that led from the great room on the left to the dining room on the right but no one was inside.

Agent Harris raised his gun toward the ceiling as he moved to get a better angle to see up the staircase, brought the weapon to attention then slowly lowered it as he recognized the two figures sitting at the top of the stairs. Harris placed his right foot onto the first step then leaned his right shoulder against the wall.

"Mr. Cole," he said almost as if saying 'hi'. He looked at the two motionless bodies near the top steps then tipped his head toward the great room. "This all you?"

Austin gave a small grin and said, "I had some help." He motioned to the young Asian sitting next to him. "I understand you may be looking for this one."

Before Harris could respond, Agent Birch came up from behind then stepped around him, holstering her weapon, and walked halfway up the stairs toward Austin. "Yes, we were."

"Where is Nick?" Austin asked before Agent Birch could continue.

"He's in the car with Mr. Daniels. He's safe."

Austin stood, stepped over the two bodies on the floor and walked down the stairs to meet her mid-way. "They're not safe until they're a long way away from here." Austin turned back to the top of the stairs and motioned for the young Asian to follow him down. Kao Yi Szun walked down the stairs and stopped beside Austin. "This is Kao Yi Szun. I think he's going to need your help and protection."

With a smile agent Birch said, "Hi," and shook the hand of Kao Yi Szun. "Are you alright?"

"Yes," was his only response.

Austin, Yi Szun and Agent Birch walked outside to the waiting black Challenger. Suddenly the passenger side door flew open and out darted Nick sprinting to intercept Austin. "Hey kid," he said, with Nick giving him a long hard hug and Stephen Daniels walking up from behind.

"So where's…" Stephen started to ask a question but Austin subtly shook his head.

Austin went through everything that happened starting with the night he'd come home from the club and ending with the confrontation only an hour earlier. After about an hour of talking through the details he summed up the issue ahead of them. "There is no way these two kids are going to be safe without your help. I think we need to talk to someone about a reliable plan to ensure their safety for a long time."

Agent Birch said, "I'll get right on it." She pulled out her phone and stepped away.

Austin turned to Yi Szun and Nick and said, "You're both going to have to trust me. I know you're not going to like this but, do what I tell you and you may come out of this alive and well." He smiled a hopeful smile and added, "It's going to be ok. It's just going to take some time."

September 22nd, 2015: Brookeland, Texas

As the sheriff's cruiser casually entered the gentle left hand curve of county road 45, the driveway to Austin's house came into view. Standing proudly in the front yard was a 'For Sale' sign seemingly inviting passersby to save it from being abandoned. Deputy Hayes pulled the cruiser into the driveway and pulled up close to Austin's pickup truck. Austin looked to be loading a tent into the back of the pickup along with some rope, a large pack that might hold sleeping bags and some other camping essentials.

"Hey, Austin," he said as he exited the cruiser.

"Hey, Jerry," replied Austin, still loading gear into his truck. "What brings you out this way?"

"I was headed over to Dempsey's place. Thought I'd swing by here and see how you're doing." Jerry walked up to the truck and rested both arms on the side board of the bed. "Looks like you're going camping. All weekend?"

"Yep. Just trying to get away from an empty house for a while," Austin said as he heaped more equipment onto the ever growing stack.

"Well, I can understand that." Jerry paused for a moment, looked around the home that he'd known as Austin's house since they were boys then took his arms off the truck. "Well, if you need someone to talk to you know where to find me." He went back to the car and opened the door and stopped. "Austin," he said, "you know that if there's anything you need, Tiffany and I are there for you. Right?"

Austin stopped what he was doing, gave Jerry a smile and said, "Of course. I just need to get away. Clear my head. I guess get prepared for changes. You know?"

Jerry nodded, gave a forced smile and said, "Sure. See you." A few moments later Jerry was driving away but carrying with him an uneasy feeling and a sense of loss.

Twenty minutes after Jerry left, Austin had finished loading up the truck, locked up the house and garage and was backing out of the driveway. He put the truck in drive and started the hour and fifteen minute drive to the hills of Nacogdoches. He couldn't help but think of Nick and how he'd gotten himself involved with Moroccan arms dealers working for Armenians.

With Nick in witness protection he'd at least have a chance at a normal life.

He kept thinking back to Agent Birch's promise to find out who the Moroccans were working for and how they'd gotten their information. Austin had left the NSA with three good sources but he doubted they'd ever talk. He knew that for arms dealers to find out about a classified DARPA program, any program, would require having someone well placed in the highest levels of government. *No way they'll be alive come time for trial,* thought Austin of the three assailants he'd left alive three months earlier in a darkened house in suburban Houston.

An hour and a half later the 2002 Ford F150 made the right turn onto the old, overgrown logging trail that led down a series of winding curves and deep drops to the rich, scenic valley below, near what used to be called Gilcrest Mill. It was a short three mile drive that took almost forty minutes to make but Austin finally pulled up next to an old tree with limbs that spread like a small shopping mall. While it was not quite 2:00 p.m. there was very little sunlight able to penetrate the many leaves and branches of the fifty foot post oak.

As he opened the door and stepped out onto the sandy dust he could see the gentle stream of water flowing lazily over shallow rock and the sound made him think of those meditation water falls you buy in department stores. He shut the door and started walking toward the stream when he caught a shadow of movement out of the corner of his left eye. He stopped in place. He lowered his head and gave a smile. "Guess you did find it," he said as he turned.

Standing there before him, about fifteen feet away holding something looking very similar to an old Geiger counter, was an attractive Asian MSS Agent known as Kao Yi Fun smiling wryly as she slowly made her way to Austin. "What took you so long?" she teased as she passed by.

"Well, I did have a few things to take care of," he said, knowing full well that she understood exactly what he had been doing. "But, I'm here now and ready to get going. The sooner we get this over with, the better. I have some unfinished business with some Armenians."

So much for weekend camping.

CPSIA information can be obtained
at www.ICGtesting.com
Printed in the USA
FFOW04n2052131214
9535FF

9 781478 738107